STORIES AND
SCENARIOS

STORIES AND SCENARIOS

Long & Short stories, Plays, Poems,
Short story scenarios

Collected works: Volume Five

MICHAEL BRAHAM GERSTEIN

To order additional copies of this book, contact:
Xlibris
800-056-3182
www.Xlibrispublishing.co.uk
Orders@Xlibrispublishing.co.uk
800922

To my good, supportive & valuable friends Priscilla, Alyson, Andrew, Dave Richman, Ann & Amelia

CONTENTS

SHORT STORIES & SCENARIOS

'SHAKING THE BLUES AWAY'

"You lying cheat. You bitch!" Flushed and shaking, he slammed the phone down! He was furious. It was over. That was it! Those were his last words to her. He gulped a Brandy, his head spinning. Lighting a cigarette, he phoned his Life Trainer. It was a long call. But it slowed him down. He felt a little cooler. He had another Brandy, then rang his theatrical agent, Robin, who was on a skiing trip in Italy.

Mel, 45, was an actor and writer. He had a solid, respectable front, which hid the usual insecurities. His marriage, was a sour, wood wormed chair of a marriage. His wife, Lesley was a beautiful, pushy drama producer, with a tongue. As a result, Mel had a mistress, Jet. More of a girl friend, because they actually talked together. And he was helping her. They met at a Book Trade Fair in Cannes. He was there, with some other writers from his publishing company. Mel specialised in novels and travel writing. But his latest book, Contemporary European Theatre and Film, was a one off. A pet project. Published a few months ago, his firm were still pushing it.

The girl friend, Jet, was a hostess employed by a large, international publishing firm. She did the information desk, book signings, served food and drink. That was 9 months ago. Mel and Lesley's marriage was in threads, and hanging by a thread, but they still shared their London town house. Separate bedrooms. Anyway, Jet preferred independence. So Mel set her up with a flat and an acting course. She was with an agency doing modelling and hospitality jobs.

1

And now, Mel had just found out that she had repaid him, by having this affair with a younger man, who was in her acting class. That was the phone call. "I set you up", Mel shouted. "I gave you a flat, your course, your monthly allowance. I thought we had something." Oh grow up", she shouted. "Of course we did, but things change don't they! Didn't you know, Mel? That's life? Get real! If you found someone better, you'd do the same. We all do. Stop accusing me, and grow up!"

Hot, indignant, crying and spluttering, he screamed down the phone at her, "You two faced, lying gold digger!" He had a failing, loveless marriage, and now she was withdrawing her love too. It was like being mugged for cash, and then having your credit card cancelled! The dam holding back his insecurities, was being bombed, and showing cracks Flesh, but emotionally, an angry, drained skeleton!

"Yes, it's an Italian / French production". Mel was chatting with his theatrical agent, Robin, on the balcony of a restaurant at Val Disere Skiing Resort. In the Italian Alps, north of Turin. "The part is for an English businessman. Filming starts at Chichivento this Spring. Try for it. It will keep you busy", Robin urged. Mel couldn't stand being in the London house on his own. Lesley was away on a production shoot. He had flown out the day after the break up. When he slammed the phone down, after finishing with Jet, he smashed books off the table, kicked over chairs, and stood by the window, crying and shaking. Still raging. Late afternoon sunlight streamed through the room. It was on him like a spotlight. He was used to stage lighting, but this disturbed him.

Theatre and films were an artificial experience. This was real life. He felt exposed. An artificial, sham life. The conflict, guilt, twisted his guts. The purity of the light on his tears and in his eyes cut like a knife.

He couldn't stand it. Choking with half sobs, gasping for breath, he turned to the phone. His desperate state fought with the pure light. That's when he rang his agent in Italy. Part of Robin's job, was to keep his client in stable emotional health, ready for jobs.

In that phone call, Robin had said, "We will go for that part, Mel. There are quite a few up for it. Its just come in. I was going to suggest it anyway. What a coincidence!"

And on the Val Disere restaurant balcony, Robin continued, "I'll set up a meeting with the producers. We will have to work on you. We'll get you ship shape with a bit of skiing, a chat with Susan, a few Martinis. Susan is the medicine you need. You know it. She's helped you before!" Susan, Robin's wife, was a journalist, an editor and ran an agony aunt column.

"Okay Robin, okay. Right. Yes." Mel shook his head, "But work? Don't know. No. I couldn't work now. Too soon. Too upset. Can't think, for God's sake, Robin. Can't think straight! God, Robin, I am so mad with her! Who can you trust? She wanted someone with more get up and go. I thought I had that, Robin. Then she says I am too safe for her! Too passive! After all this time, it's just dawned on her? Who is she kidding. She was just after my money. And my help. This new bloke she's got. She says he's got more edge, more risk. He's more macho. She said that's what she needs. Oh, it's just dawned on her, has it? And she dumps on me, the bitch"

"Mel, come on man, we all dump on each other". Robin said, "That's life. Everyone is out for themselves. We're all still cavemen!" "Yes Robin. Yes. Yes, okay. You're right. Your right. Its those demons again. Emotional deprivation. Can't take rejection. You know it all. You know how fragile I am. It's like having all the goodies in a room, and then having the door slammed in your face!" "Mel, you know I know". Robin coaxed his man, like a trainer getting his fighter ready. "Mel, how about a few days in Skyros? Bit of Yoga, Meditation. Your inner man.... ...you know. You liked it last year. Take a break. You worked very well on the Theatre and Film book. You enjoyed that last film. It's been a good year".

"Right. Not bad at all. Maybe. Actually, now I am over here, you know what I'd love to do? You know. Find that house. You remember, Guerechi's place, in the Po valley. You know, the Don Camillo author."
"Okay, that's good too", Robin encouraged his client and friend.
"God Robin, you know, I just love European Culture. It stirs me up. I am really going to enjoy this new book". Mel had got the publisher to give the go ahead for a new project. One close to his heart. Mel had already begun research. The working title was, 'The Pets Project'. There would be the standard T.V. documentary and book.

He was going to cover some of his own favourite creative people ['Pets'] across all the arts. Some in America. Most in Europe. He wanted to begin with Bach, through Beethoven, Vienna, Goethe and the Weimar Republic, Chopin, and Paris, Brahms, the French and Russian writers. Sibelius, The Impressionists. But concentrating on the period he loved the most. The early 20th century art movements and experiments. Chagall and Picasso. Django Reinhardt, Eisenstein, Rossellini, Fellini...... He would film the places where they lived and worked. Plus American entertainment: Cole Porter, The Gershwins, Fred Astaire, Judy Garland, Gene Kelly... He was already researching for an interview with Betsy Blair, Gene Kelly's first wife, who was living in London.

"What about Lesley", Robin asked, lighting a cigar. What will happen? Any idea yet?"
"You know, Robin, after that phone call, while I was in all that pain, you know, raging, I felt I had to clear the air, clear my conscience, lay it out, and tell Lesley about Jet. God I still feel so awful! Now Jet is out, I feel clear to square it with Lesley. I have got to jump in, let go. Like a parachutist. Better jump, than to hold it in".
"Good Mel. Like I always said, you should have told her ages ago. But as long as you get it out your system. But wait till she is back from her shoot".
"Yes, of course. This is it Robin. It will shake the mountain and start an avalanche.
I will either be crushed under, or the gates will open. I got enough to think about till she gets back. By the way, did I tell you I began a letter to that bitch, Jet? What I think of her! Let some poison out. Yes. It's in the style of a poem. I began it on the plane over".
"Show it to me before you send it, Mel"
"Sure. And I've got to write to Lesley as well. It's funny, Robin, but Jet always mentioned Sinatra as her ideal man. Hu. Doubt it. If only she knew the reality. What a dreamer. Bloody bitch dreamer!" His curse died on the air, like a soldier cut down.

"Hi guys". Robin's wife, Susan, waved and bounced on to the balcony. A close friend, Jeanette, was with her. "It was great", Susan grinned.

"The snow was good?", Robin asked. "It was all good", Susan laughed, "The snow, the air, the run, everything. Wasn't it Jean?" Jeanette tossed her long brunette hair in agreement.

Mel liked Susan. Stable and motherly on one hand. Sharp and competitive on the other. She was a magazine editor. She ran the Features section of a woman's magazine, with Jeanette. She specialised in Gossip and relationships. Susan did the agony aunt column. Mel had sometimes talked over his relationship problems with her. Both she, and of course Robin knew about his affair with JET. Susan was a hustler. Her eyes could change from warm understanding, to ruthless, mustard keen. Clint's eyes. A gunslinger's eyes. An English rose with thorns! In the bitchy, media world, she was able to retain her fairly calm, realistic balance. Jeanette was Susan's P.A., and also helped with the advice column. He was going to need a chat with Susan, about the break up.

"You know Robin", Susan continued, "Jeanette and I decided we must go and see Phil. You know his yacht is in St. Raphael, this week. Lets pop down for a few days. We can stay on board. Or we could stay at Ronnie's. At the vineyard. Of course you come, Mel".
"Phone them Robin", Susan urged. "We were going to try this year's new vintage, weren't we. We haven't been for months, have we?".
"Okay", Robin agreed. "Last summer. Last year. Went to that open air Jazz Festival".
"Right? Ronnie's place is just outside, what's that village, that arty, touristy place? Chiavari, or something.

Mel got up and leaned on the balcony. It looked over a cluster of chalets in the snow. The image echoed a feeling of how his friends were clustering together around him, now. His film hero, James Cagney. What would he do in Mel's situation? Go for a ski? Bury his head in the snow? Go and punch Jet's new boy friend? Scream or stay close to his friends? At decision times, he would sometimes flash imagine what other heroes would do, real and fiction. But Cagney was his main man.

"Robin, you remember those musicians we met at the Jazz Festival last year?" Mel heard Susan making arrangements behind him. "You are still in touch aren't you? Let's see if they can come over to Ronnie's. They are locals, aren't they?

That night, in his guest chalet, drenched with Brandy, Mel finished the poisoned letter / poem he had begun. He had had enough of direct confrontations with Jet.

But there was juices of poison to get out. As he wrote, he saw those 18th century doctors draining patients of blood and water to get rid of poisons and infections.

He was a poison draining writer. It was slightly less painful this way. He needed some therapeutic release. But he wouldn't send the letter. The poem was coming out in the antique style. He had done a few Shakespeare plays, and this classical format helped to neutralise the pain a little. Take the edge off. This is the letter / poem:

'A Fool in Love' or 'A Fall in Love'

Madam, my love for you has now decreased,
Along with my support cheques,
Which now have ceased!
Please receive last payment,
With some perfume, to one who was 'heaven scent'.
A 'final pay off' and thank you,
To a lady I once trusted, once knew!

Last night I was choking
Over that trust, so cruelly broken.
You calmly said,
"I've been seeing another man.
I'm phoning from his bed!"
Right behind my back, you, you… 'also ran'!
I am choked by your news.
Choked that I must lose!
And now, in whose bed are you reading this?
Whose lips now receive your kiss!
Oh boy, have I been led,
Right up the garden path!
More than 'murder most foul'
You have been with him, cheek by jowl.
While so called, loving me.
Oh out, out, dam treachery!

And what about this past year,
While I paid for your acting career?
You had my full support.
You fought for it.
"It was important", you cried.
You lied, lied you!
Another lie to join the queue!
So, instead of acting lessons,
You attended other kinds of dramatic sessions!
Instead of your class in ballet dance,
You had other kinds of dalliance!

As smooth as silk
You have been seeing him.
Your scruples are curdled milk!
If you had come clean,
Confessed to my face,
Had the grace to say, "I'm sorry".
I could have chucked my rage on the back of a lorry,
And put it behind me.

But now, be assured,
I will become inured
To your behaviour
To a heart deeply injured.
Now I hate the day that your
Life became entwined with mine.

Now I see you are self centred.
You bitch, I hope you die!
You are also, big headed!
Pig headed....oh God, why, oh why!

I doted on you.
I could see
I would have asked you to marry me.
But now I see, you are full of hypocrisy
Go and drown in the sea!
I've got to drown my misery!

I am sure your latest 'him'
Will be your next victim!
You must enjoy your power over men.
You are like the rest.
Like the police on a false arrest.
You like that sense of power.
You are all a cold hearted shower!
But go rain on someone else.
Preferably, go and wet yourself!

You are now out of bounds.
But remember, no fox, no hounds.
Found your next victim to make ill?
Found your next prey to hunt and kill?
Found another one to hang and dry?
Shakespeare had it right.
It's 'dog eat dog'.
Well, this is one dog who is going to fight!
But I'll probably love you till I die!

You are like all the media.
They build you up, then feed ya
To the wolves!
Why are men such gullible fools?
Fall in love and you're a gonna!
Why trust a woman's word and honour?
When they are just a smiling Lucrecia Borgia!

That night, Mel had a dream. He was in a Cagney film. Mel was playing Cagney's character. The hoodlum, gangster, with a family, and a conscience.

He is there, with his mother, and all the gang. They are finishing a meal of pasta bolognaise. They way Mamma makes it. Smoking and drinking, they are discussing a crisis. They found out someone's been squealing to a rival outfit. Snitching secret information. About Mel! He has a piece on the side. Jet, a model. His wife, Lesley, she don't know. Mel wipes the sauce off his mouth with a hairy hand and speaks. "This information, in the wrong hands, it could smash our organisation. If the papers hear of it, or the Unions...... We gotta find the snitch, so he don't talk no more.

And we gotta silence the Porkenaisse's. We been watching them, right Rosco?
You and Begasso. You found out, eh. They trying to muscle in on our operation, on the North side, eh. They gotta be dealt with, yes? Yes Ma?"

"When I finds out who is double crossed my boy, they'll pay in Hell!" Ma spits out.
"We all agrees then". Mel wasn't asking, he was telling.
The phone rang, one of those tall black hook numbers.
Roscoe answers. "For you Ma".
Ma takes the call. It was short. She goes to the head of the table, looking furious.
"That was our 'grass', Eddie, from the North side. He's just seen Gambinni. He's found out who the squealer is". Tears in her eyes she fixes an angry stare on Mel.
"My own son, you swine! You double crossing, lying snake. My son. A son of mine!"
Mel fingers his gun. "Have I ever lied to you, Ma?" Mel protested.
"Not me Ma, it wasn't..........Not me........."

At this point Mel woke up. He couldn't take any more of the dream. It was too pointed. He was sweating with guilt. Keeping guilty secrets, like mistresses, even though it was over, was as good as a workout. Mel had another slug of brandy.

Next morning, he was feeling so insecure, he rang his Broker, and sold his low risk shares!
After breakfast, the four friends went for a long ski. Mel was ahead of the others.
He hit a steep snow cliff and went down at 40mph. The rush of air and snow spray savaged his face and played havoc with his breathing. He was on the edge of control, just coping with the buffeting, his body stronger from recent exercise. But, he was out of control, emotionally, over this recent buffeting. His mind was still speeding too. Why had Jet left him for some hunk? Some skunk of a hunk! The others were some way behind, but still in his slip stream. The downhill levelled off now to a flatter run. The scritch, scrunch of skis, the intense white of snow, even through goggles, the bushes, trees, boulders whirling by, the wind rush, the taut, sharp air...... he was bombarded with a kaleidoscope of images.

His chaotic state identified. Ahead, birds were gliding on smooth air currents. Contentment and Jonathan Livingston Seagull came to mind, and his eyes moistened.

Both inside and out was chaotic and churning. He glanced at the sky. It was on the move, unstable. He looked at the ski run ahead. He turned his head to see his friends still behind. And felt reassured a bit. But still felt so god dammed angry with everything. He knew it was an indulgence. But hell, if he can't have a tantrum now.....Jesus, people do far worse things.....The cracks in the dam got bigger. He even felt a failure, though somewhere, rationally, he knew he wasn't. Mel felt that he never had really achieved his dreams..... Rat a tat tat.....One disturbing thought after another, as he hurtled down. The noise of the skiis, the air pressure, the trees flashing by, the electric blue sky crushing down on him, increased the almighty inner crescendo. His whole orchestra was playing out of tune, and in different tempos.

Now he was shaking his fist at fate, like Beethoven. God, and everyone he knew, were wrong about him. He had failed. Certainly, a failed marriage. Now he heard familiar thoughts: "It's my life. I'll do what I like. I'll kill myself on my birthday, just to spook everyone. I'll get my own back on the bastards. Another recurring thought flashed by. Then he imagined himself burying his head under a pile of autumn leaves in a deserted field outside Rome. To commune, close to nature. It was a recurring image. He wanted to both hide away, secretly, and decide what to do next with his life. But he dismissed that thought. Too tame for now. Then a golden oldie hit him hard, like a pile driver. They were still high up, on the mountain. For one moment, for one moment in his life, he thought of the thrill, the exhilaration, of doing some thought free, knife edge action. Of letting go, completely. Even if it was the last one. The ultimate. To let go his life. He wanted, desperately, to let his skies veer off the run and over the edge.

And it was just then, that he began to feel a kind of vibration inside him. It felt warm yet urgent. It began by itself. He became aware of it. It was intense. All through him. And he realised, clearly, that it was his own nature at work. Somehow, some healing power had been triggered off. An inner healing was at work, clearing out his poison. Like the immune system kicking out unwanted, foreign bodies. All the things that were not really him. It was the opposite of repression! He felt like the Pompidou Museum, exposed, everything exposed and visible to view. All his feelings, thoughts, pain, personality, the real him and the false one. He could no longer hide them from anyone.

His whole body screamed out to be free of his English inhibitions. To let go of it all. Like a boil that's desperate, aching to burst. The vibration continued on by itself. It was helping him relax. To sink back, supported, as if in idyllic warm waters. One quiet Sunday morning, he had sat in a secluded park, an oasis, by a small lake. In brilliant Spring sunshine. He surrendered to the breathless stillness. He wasn't thinking. And he didn't want to. His body needed more. More of the same. Mel remembered how he had felt, standing by the window, after that phone call. There seemed to be two vibration signals, giving off two different colours. One for his real self, and one for the false. Gradually the vibration stopped.

And Mel knew, just how many years of repression there were still to be shaken loose.
He had heard that Transcendental Meditation did something similar. Pure Vibrations released stress from the nervous system.

A friend had a dog. He said, "not only is the dog my best friend, but also, better than any therapist!". He said "Doggie is always just himself. Did his own thing in his own way. And each breed of dog has its own individual ways. Like an elephant. An elephant does not try to behave like an ant. Can you imagine a load of elephants trying to make an ant hill! Mel instinctively knew that the vibration he had felt, was working to take out the 'undoggie' in him, so he could be the real 'doggie' he really, already was.

And then, he felt imaginary Waters rushing around his body, to cool him. He gasped, and his eyes filled. He blinked them dry. And in a blink, the feelings changed. The Waters began to bubble. Now he was vibrating with excitement! He looked up and screamed! He yelled! The relief was tangible. Weeks of poison leached out. He sped by some bushes, and peach coloured petals, gossamer thin, serenaded into the blue. The sunlight sparked through them, like a hymn. Mel chased up in prayer, up after the petals.

All of this took about 5 minutes. But also, a lifetime. At the end of their ski break, they decided to drive to the Riveira coast. They had friends there. Ronnie and Phil had to put them off till next week. They had guests. Phil was entertaining business partners on his boat.

The four, Mel, Robin, Susan and Jeanette, drove to Monte Carlo, and arrived in the evening. The Marina was lit up, like a brilliant musical show. The lights were dazzling and dancing from the moored boats. A shimmering kaleidoscope in the navy, black velvet night. Mel found the breath taking scene hard to take. He was more aware of the blackness than the lights. He identified more with the black night than the dancing lights. His raw, bloodied emotions crawled off, into bed. In fact, there was a fun fair down by the Marina. Even in off season.

They parked, and wandered lazily down the hill, through gardens to the Fun Fair. It was too late to stay with friends, a middle age English couple. So they went to a hotel they knew. Spent morning in Monte. Then late afternoon, with the English couple, they went along the Middle Corniche, in two cars, to Nice. More friends there, who had a holiday home. Stopped at Eze. Medieval town perched high on the mountains.

Drove down to the little beach at foot of cliffs. Walked with Jeanette, away from others.
Moon reflected on sea. The evening cool, but not chill. No sea breeze. Coastal lights of Cap Ferrat. Again Mel felt that uneasy conflict for third or fourth time in a week. The place nature, innocent, pure. His feelings an ugly, diseased can of worms. The sea splashing swirling around the rocks echoed his chaotic feelings.

Being close to Jeanette, a pretty, understanding, warm person, felt like a bandage across the wound. Then he began to feel the inner vibration again. That's when he realised, he could not consciously make the vibration happen. It was his nature at work. When he wanted to be relaxed, real and open. Being near to person like Jeanette, helped. They sat on some flat rocks. Robin and Susan knowingly, left Mel alone, and wandered together, along the beach.

The dazzling moon's reflection, shimmered on the black sea. It seemed, to Mel, almost proud, narcissistic. The shimmering was a visual mirror of his inner vibration. A quilted, velvet incandescence. All mixed together. He could half see blue angels flying in the evening sky. Like a Chagall He had seen a film about angels helping people, by a Polish director.

The sea, the evening, the calm, still air, the brilliant reflected moon, and being with Jeanette, triggered it all off. The vibration and the feelings.
"You know Jeanette", Mel said, "I do all this writing, and acting. All part of the entertainment business. Your Magazine too. I don't know. It might be this place making me feel this way. But I have often thought that entertainment is an artificial way of simulating what we would like to feel, but find hard. You know, a kind of nourishment.

Oh, dam it!" At last Mel let rip. "Oh bloody hell. You know, those times we feel full, even happy, and you have to let it out in some way, share it with friends". Jeanette just had time to blurt out, "Yes, I know what you're getting at."

Mel quickly went on. "That's what I'm talking about. That moon and the air, it's bringing it out of me. You know with certain people, you can relax, and enjoy their company. Others you can't. That's what everyone wants to feel. Men, women, anyone!

You know, the pleasure stuff. The buzz stuff. You know when you feel something open inside. Like some deep perfumed, blood red flower, bursting open in your chest. Like it fills you up. Like in a gas station; "Fill her up with some good stuff matey. Unleaded." That's what everybody wants. Entertainment, it's like drugs and drink. When you don't have the real macoy, well you got to have something or you could feel yourself getting desperate, or crazy! Don't you?"

"I know what you mean", Jeanette said warmly, with a little giggle. "I'm with you. I mean, what you are talking about is like, nourishment. And when you don't have that, well, people go worse than crazy. We are all looking for that sort of, stimulation. With friends too.

"That's it. And that's proof", Mel went on, "that all that artificial pleasure stuff, well, it's like a simulation of the real thing. It is proof of the absence of real feelings. From the heart. Oh God, Jeanette". Mel flung his arms around Jeanette's neck, broke down and cried. "Sorry. I can't help it. That girl has hurt me badly. Big time".

Mel was shaking and sobbing. Jeannette patted him. But then, she suddenly shook him by the shoulders, angry.
"Hey, Mel. Come on, for God's sake. What goes on? You know what goes on. You know the game. Stop the self pity. Stop indulging. I bet Jet wasn't the first girl. What about your wife? She didn't even know about Jet. You've never told her? She's in the dark! Come on man, you know the score".
"Oh God. Right. Okay. Yea", Mel spluttered, wiping tears with back of hand, and sucked in evening air. "No, yes, okay, right, no, I mean there was another girl before Jet.
Yes, you are right. But she's really stitched me. Okay....okay. No. Yes. You are right, but...." Still holding him by the shoulders, Jeanette looked straight at Mel.
"You know there's pain. That's life! That's Poker. What's the song... 'I've played, I've won and lost....or, no, that other one.....'Now I'm taking the game up, and the Ace of Hearts is high'. Remember?" She knew Mel was into his music.

Mel gulped in air. This woman saw it black and white. But then she worked on Personal Pages of a Women's magazine. A cutthroat profession at best. A Poker face, a little bluffing, and a little hustling come in handy. She knew the way the game plays from all angles. And tears cut no ice in a Poker game.
Black Mediterranean waves rolled in, slewshing on the sand. Mel felt an inner flow.
Rhythmically in tune with the waves. Jeanette's voice, her presence, the hypnotic sound of the water, whatever, he wanted to let go of the pain.
"Jeanette, I got that vibrating movement again. You know, inside me. I told you. I can feel it, again, right now." Mel had told Jeanette, about it, earlier. About his experience on the ski slopes.

"Relax, Mel, and let it happen. Just sit and be. Don't think". Jeanette held his hand.

The movement got stronger, and turned into that familiar vibration. The lapping of the waves seemed to him, like a kind of midwife, encouraging birth. He let the vibration do its thing for few minutes. The moon shone innocently. The urge was to purge, to purify.

When the vibrating stopped, Mel stayed where he was for a while, recovering.

Then he and Jeanette got up and walked across the beach to the others.

"Milan won. Just got the score on text. 2-1". Robin showed Mel his mobile. "Oh you didn't know about the game". Susan tossed her hair at Robin, and let out an "Oh God!", and gave Mel and Jeanette an understanding look.

They crunched up the beach to the cars and drove on to Nice. They arrived late evening, and went to their friends house. It was in a posh quarter of Nice, on a hill, just near the Chagall Biblical Museum. Then they went out for a meal. The English couple had to stay with friends of theirs. There wasn't enough sleeping room in the house. So the English couple stayed with friends. They chatted, watched some T.V., and then went to bed. Mel was in his room, when he heard the others, downstairs, talking loudly. He thought they were all in bed. He went down. They were round the T.V., and when they saw Mel they began shouting.

"It's on the news!", Robin was furious. "You bastard! You knew about this, didn't you?"

"What?" Mel was in shock. "What's going on?"

"She's been murdered!", Susan shouted.

"Who?". Mel was scared and shaking.

"Who? You really mean you don't know", Robin shouted.

"What's going on. Tell me!"

"It's on the news. Jet has been murdered!". Now Susan was hitting Mel.

"Oh god, no. Susan stop it! Oh god, no. You don't mean it? Susan stop it. What's the matter with you".

Jeanette was sobbing. Their friends were dumbstruck.

"You'll have to really convince me you didn't know about this, Mel", Robin shouted.

"It said a young model was found dead in London. Name, Jet. A middle age woman was arrested. Name, Lesley......
Mel, screamed out, "No, no. Oh my god, no, no, no, no! What's happening? It can't be!"

"It said the arrested woman had gone to the police and confessed", Susan shouted. "You said you hadn't told Lesley about Jet. You liar, Mel. You filthy liar. Look what you've done!"

"Robin went up to Mel. "Look me in the face, and tell me you had nothing to do with it. Look me in the face and tell me you and Lesley didn't plot this together!".

"Robin, Susan, I don't know anything about it. I'm in shock. For god sake! Lesley doesn't know about Jet. I haven't told her yet. She never knew. I was going to tell her but...."
"All that self pity", Jeanette shouted accusingly. "Crying on my shoulder. This is your fault. You're the guilty one here!"

Robin shouted, "I wash my hands of you Mel. You and me are finished. What torment Lesley must have been in to do this! You said you would wait before you told Lesley!
You lied to me, Mel. You lied. God fancy telling her like that! What happened to the letter you were going to write to Lesley? I'm phoning the police about this. You are as guilty as Lesley! You drove her to it!"
Jeanette, the English couple were all screaming at Mel. Susan was still hitting him.

Robin was on the phone. "Hello, police.........
Mel was shouting out as he woke up. He lurched up in the bed, sweating.

He'd had a nightmare. The T.V. news, the murder, Lesley, his wife, the accusations.... He'd been dreaming. A nightmare. A guilty nightmare? God, was he relieved!

He got up, still shaking, and went on to the balcony. He looked up at the night sky. The moon seemed almost sympathetic now. And he thought he saw the stocky figure of Jimmy Cagney waving from the night sky, and shouting at him, "Top of the world Mel. Top of the world!"

TOUGHENING UP

My Grandmother suddenly turned on me. "You are too soft. You've got no discipline. And it' s too late. The damage is done." She went on relentlessly, "You're mother has spoiled you. She has been too soft with you... You won't change".

She had an upright, Victorian manner, which gave her steely authority. I was painting her portrait at the time. I was studying Art and Design. I was shocked, crushed, hurt and embarrassed, all at the same time. Believe me, it is possible. "Ruby!". My grandmother looked over my shoulder, and called out, "Ruby, you know what his problem is? you have been too soft with him". Ruby, my mother, was in the kitchen. She came in. "You have spoiled him". My Grandmother spoke over my head this time. "He wont be able to do anything with his life now. He won't get anywhere!. He hasn't got what it takes. And its too late!", my grandmother spoke in a clear, sensible way. But she spoke as if I were not there! I never finished her portrait.

I brooded for days. No one spoke to me about it, or told me how to get tougher. In the days after, I suffered hopeless feelings. They felt surgically implanted in my guts.

The adventurous, happy blue skies, that should have been mine, were not there. Grey clouds were parked in my heart. Illegally. A heavy Yorkshire pudding thudded across the horizon. I saw my life. I was 25. Stuck at home. A mum's boy!

A few days later, I packed a bag, and went to the front door. My father stood there. "Where are you going?", he demanded. My

mother had already told him. "I am leaving home", I was a bundle of nerves. I tried to put my case. "I can't take any more. I am getting nowhere. My father's arm gestures clearly said, "No way!" "Where is he going? What is he doing? My mother tried to explain calmly. "He feels he cant go on like this. He wants to stand on his own feet." Then, I told him what my grandmother had said.
"I am leaving. Grandma was right. I am too soft. I've got to go out in the world and get tougher. I can't do it at home. I cant go on like this.
I've got to fight and get a home for myself". My father was outraged. "You have a home here. You have got everything here. You are not going! Over my dead body!" He was upset and offended... He seemed to care. I was too weak and gave in.

The following year, my hand was forced. Still soft. No tougher. I was steamed up; a force of nature. I imagine a swollen river flooding to the sea, would have the same kind of urgency that I had now. I had to become a someone! I packed a bag, and left home that afternoon. I only told my mother. No idea what my father said when he found out. I made my way to Kings Cross, for the cheap hotels. The story had begun. Youth leaves home to make his fortune.

First test, slay the Dragon. Kings Cross Station could have been my Dragon. Fire and smoke billowed up into the air. Into the slate blue sky, streaked with blood orange from a setting sun. This was the days of steam trains. The noise from train whistles, shouts, passengers in the station, the searing noise of the traffic, crowds of people fighting to walk in the streets, gave the whole scene a look of Armageddon proportions.

This was my first challenge. To tough it out and not run home.
I thought I had done enough for one day. But no! I was not done. Watching people rushing about, I was aware I was in a furnace. Red hot. Flames were shooting up, burning into me. The heat was on. The embarrassing gap between my softness and these people's toughness, that was the heat I was feeling. A test. Give me a test. I want to prove my manhood. (that doesn't look so good in print.!) A test. Not a hollow 'rites of passage' celebration. I need something really courageous. Those manhood tests young men have to do, in primitive tribes, in the jungles. that's the sort of thing. I think they leap off tall trees. And end up very short men. And they

have to kill animals with spears. That would liven up a Barmitzvah! Instead of a speech, make the boy leap off the synagogue roof. Better still, the Rabbi. Probably have to change the line, "Today I am a man" to, "Today I am a cripple"

I look around Kings Cross for a jungle or some tall trees. I was pacing up and down now, really fed up. Flexed muscles, some victory under belt, a notch on a gun all came to mind. A pub. Get drunk, pick a fight. That would do it. I get out of that one. Remember, don't drink. I am too soft, cant hold alcohol. I could attack passengers going into the station. Take a wild chance. Could I be in a worse state. Probably end up in court. Jail?
Pick up a girl. That would do it. Would I dare? I was walking around in a garden near Euston station now. Desperate, crazy, I crossed the motorway, aimlessly. I walk past the columns of female Caryatids outside the church. I begin to chat to them, to flirt. I beg them to come for a coffee. They tell me to get lost! Their mute indifference echoes all London.

I began to run in short bursts, then walk, paced around gardens, sat on benches, head in hands. Tried to talk to passers by. I was willing myself, daring myself. It felt like the front line of a war. I am past desperation now. I am getting delirious.
Then as I walked past St. Pancras Station, #Zing, Ping. I heard this MUSIC in my head. Loud, Triumphal sort of stuff.
Then suddenly, the station reared up and turned into a giant monster robot, huge and menacing. Trains flew off the rails up into the sky. I ran across the road and down into the vast hole left by the station. I was in the station cellar. The music played in my ears. It was a strange place. The music lifted me, and suddenly, breathlessly, I was flying through a labyrinth of tunnels. I passed monsters and strange creatures, laughing, screaming. But I knew as I flew, that I had that strength, confidence to do anything I wanted. It was my first sign of the inner battle to come. The battle to change.

In this emotional imagining were metaphors / creatures that express; anger, frustration. humiliation, fear of death, closed heart, bitterness, tantrums, bile, stuck, fight to change, walls, resents, paralysis, soft, spoilt, no real love, need to open heart, to let go of negatives. To find your own voice, body and soul; fight to change, win spurs, win tests, get tougher, and hopes to change.

It had been a DAYDREAM. I hit the ground and snapped awake. I felt the hard, grey pavement again. The music had stopped. I looked around, still in shock. St. Pancras Station was back to its usual shape.

The slate blue sky, smudged with dark grey, and threaded with highlights, reflected my mood. Went to McDonalds. Shared a table with a man called Harry. He was about 50, casually dressed. He had keen eyes, and a kind, intelligent face. He was friendly, so I told him what I was up to. "I've left home. I've got to learn to stand on my own feet, and build my confidence. Harry eyed me and said, "At your age you are jumping in the deep end. I learned to stand on my own two feet soon as I left school. I was 14 and got local job. Worked hard. Had to. No Benefits then. Soon made me worldly and tough. You, you are born soft middle class. Got benefits to fall back on. Never done any real hard graft, have you? That is no way to build your confidence, is it. That is no way to flex your muscles and toughen up". Harry's eyes, sharp and observant, flicked around the café and back to me. He fingered his tea cup. "You see, you have been shielded from life, from hard knocks".

Now, Harry looked at me with genuine empathy. "Soft, your grandma. said, didn't she". But it was not your fault". "No?". I felt that catch of breath before tears. Harry didn't stop. "Do you see. You born into all of it. But there is more to it". "Oh no", I moaned. I shifted uneasily in my seat and gulped some tea. Harry went on, "You have had some powerful traumatic shock... I can tell. It is clear". "Are you a therapist?", I asked. "No. I just observe. I have seen it in people before. You have had some experience of fear. A lot of terrible fear. And it is all still stuck inside you. It is like a Big Mac stuck inside, that you can't digest. And it has been giving you terrible pain, for most of your life".

"I must get tougher". My wet eyes and half gasp now mixed with desperate impatience. Harry looked around and then eyed me. I told him, "I have got to get a job". I nearly banged the table. But to get any job, I need to be tougher and more confidence than I am. And if it is so hard to get a job, how can I get stronger?"

Harry patted my hand. and said, "At your age, you have to do it by small steps".
You should have started younger, like me, like I said. To really live, you got to get stuck in, be involved. Be busy, always moving.

You seen a swimmer. What is he in?" I watched Harry's eyes. "He's in water", I replied gingerly. Right. Water is what he works with. His body feels the water, as he moves about. It's palpable. Very different feeling to being on dry land. Or a painter. What does he work with?" "Paints. That sort of thing you mean?", I questioned. "Yes, Harry nodded. "Very different feeling using paints, to someone swimming. With paint, you feel the paints with your nerves, in your guts, and you move them around the paper as you feel, making changes here and there. Living is like that. And living is made to be used in its own special way. It is not made to be a spectator, just watching, or holding your breath and trying to hide away. You got jump in. Like the people here in McDonalds. Like that girl on her own over there. Get busy with others, moving, changing....... .... But you know all this. Sorry. We just got to get you tougher".

"Yes, Harry. It is really nice of you to help me like this. What a stroke of luck bumping into you". "Luck? Harry chuckled to himself. "Luck?. No well, its nice to have some company. But the point is that you are so soft, it will be hard to get the momentum going... So you got to practice doing small things first. You are already finding it hard, because you are not used to it". I glanced around at the tables, and agreed.
"It was all I could do to get of my house. I don't know if I have the get up and go to even practice. I've got so much resistance". "Okay. Okay. what does an athlete do? He has to train in small ways. Gets up cold days. Hard to force himself. What makes him do it.? He has a goal. To get fitter faster. You are lost now. You want to get fitter. There is somewhere you want to go. Do you give up? You do what you have to. Ask. Get a map. Go forward, go back get lost. So what. Long as you get stuck in, involved. And it depends. How much do you want it. Want to give up smoking or drinking? Depends. If you really want to. Then you will do what it takes" "Is that why its taking so long for me. I don't want it enough?", I wondered. Harry pointed to his cup. "No excuses, my friend. Get me another tea, will you".

I mulled all this over, and when I got back to the table, I asked Harry, "So, to do something, I don't really want to do, even though I do really, I have to fool myself by doing small jobs, every day, so the something I want, builds up, gradually. So I sort of don't notice I am slowly doing the something that I don't want to do, but really do. So I have to quietly do it, by not realising that I am doing it? Is it something like that?" "A bit, yes, a bit", Harry said. "Soon as you feel the resistance, you wont practice. So, you got to be like a burglar. Softly, softly catches the monkey". "Oh, I said dryly, So you got to be soft in order to stop being soft". "Yes, very good, but you got to watch yourself. You will try anything not to practice. Any excuse to not do the thing you really want to.

I know it sounds odd. It seems I had to creep up on myself with small steps, in order to make the change with small steps, to avoid not taking the small steps that I need to take, to achieve what I want and at the same time, don't want. Like a smoker. You do and you don't. My Confidence level rose to 3/100. My confusion level went to danger!

Harry said, "Right, you have heard what I think. You see now, I want to help you. Do you trust me?" "What?" I was surprised. "Do you trust me. What do you think", Harry asked. "Well, yes I do trust you". "Fine", Harry went on. "Go over to that girl, and chat to her. She is pretty, and she's on her own". "I couldn't", I protested. I don't have enough confidence". "You trust me?" Harry persisted. "Well, yes", I replied. "Time for some practice. Go over to her. I'll give you a line. It never fails". If you don't try, I will leave you, right here and now!" I got up and sat down at the girl's table. Gave her the line. "I had to get away from that man over there". I nodded towards Harry. "It certainly is nicer here", and, amazingly, she became friendly. I felt a warm door open. She was a Pro. And waiting for her friend and manager. We chatted. "Why are you so tense?", she asked. "What's wrong?" I am on a trip to change and I have just started". I told her very briefly about my challenge.

"I can let you have some drugs. That shoiuld help", she offered. "No, thanks", I said. "This trip I have got to do by myself, without help like that", I told her, bravely. "Or, you can call me", she suggested. I've got a job soon, but I can see you later on tonight. Here is my card". "Okay, thanks. I'll see". Thanks for being so nice".

I stood up. Harry is watching me. And now, there is a young man with him.

I get up for another tea. A couple of young guys came in, knocked into me, laughed, and spilt my tea. Then they began to pester the girl. #Wow no cow tow. I heard that MUSIC again. No daydream this time. For real, but inspiring. I began to hit the men and punched them out into the street. (Fight in café. I win) The girl kissed and thanked me. "Wow. Awesome. Maybe you can do it without drugs" "You know, being with you... ...you've inspired me." The girl's friend / manager came in. He thanks me. They both left for work. I had her card. # Hear Love Above MUSIC I DAYDREAM again. I climb up stairway to sky. Flew. Surfed waves in sky with other youths and lovely creatures. Elation, joy. Some mercenary soldiers came at me I had gun. Shot them all. I leapt on horse and flew thro. clouds and walls. Off the horse into a flying boat. Dropped down fast into ocean. Play with fish and mermaids. (Esther Williams.) Fly boat up to sky again and down to the sea again, and suddenly, drop in to seat, back in McDonalds. The Daydream is over.

I go back to Harry's table. "First few tests, and you did them all", he remarks warmly.
Meet Danny, a friend". He is the young man I saw before. Harry leaned forward. "Danny has a proposition for you. I encourage you to accept it. It will be more good practice. Danny spoke. "I am an ecologist working from University on research project. But I have a package that needs delivering in Paris. And I am too busy. Harry says you are free. Would you? I will pay you". "I need all the practice now I can get", I told him. What's the package, Danny?"
"It is an artist's original painting which is going to a printer in Paris to be turned into a Lithograph Edition. The artist is a friend. And he can't go either. It can't go by post. It is too valuable". Now Harry looked at me with those keen, bright eyes. "Remember, you trust me. I am helping you" "Yes Harry", I nodded...

"Okay. Well, the reality is this. Danny is an arms dealer. That ecology is just a cover. Hidden in the painting is a microfilm. It contains an arms deal order. A big one. This is one way Danny does it. Using a courier. Here is the Paris address. It is a printers, which is also a cover. Take the Eurostar tomorrow morning. Check into a cheap hotel. Stay a few days. Enjoy yourself... It is all part of your practice. And I will see you here again in 4 days. And I will be here. Trust me. I am on your case". Danny said to me, "Harry is genuine, believe me. He will help you to get where you want. Guess what, he did it for me". I told them both, "This is like a dream. I'm trying to trust you." The more you trust, Danny said, "the more you will feel you belong. And you will only really understand that the more you trust Harry".

Here is the painting, in this folder. Take care of it. And yourself. Watch, look around you. We have competitors everywhere who would like our business". And Harry just said, "The rest of the evening is yours. See you here in 4 days". They got up. I followed. As they went out the door, Harry banged into a large man coming in. Deliberately. The large man swore, "Oy, you bloody idiot, I'll smack you for that!" Harry turned and shouted, "You bloody idiot. It wasn't me, it was him. Harry pointed at me, winked, and they left. The large man swung at me. I heard that triumphal music. We fought in the café and I beat him. Left with the painting.

I rang girl. Told to wait till she finished a job. Booked in to a cheap hotel. Walked around, went to bar. Then went round to her, quite late. Stayed the night. Dreamt. Fight with thugs; defending girl again. Become a frightening grotesque monster, like a devil. Start to conquer world. Wipe out many people by eating them. Become a dictator; head of mafia; a football thug leader. Wake early sweating. But confidence levels up. Get busy. Leave girl... Check out of hotel which I never stayed in. Me and painting take Eurostar to Paris. Breakfast on train. Coming out of the toilet, I notice couple of suited guys watching me down the corridor. I thought, if this arms order was the big time, then these guys might be carrying. I remember Danny telling me to watch out. I quickly return to my carriage and hide behind a seat. I heard the two men come in, and not seeing me begin to run out again. At that point I stuck out a leg, and the men fell headlong over. I pulled the communication cord. The train screeched to a halt.

"They did it I shouted out". Other passengers helped me hold the men down. The guards came in. I and some other passengers agree that the men pulled the cord on purpose. The two men were arrested, and despite their protests, were taken off the train at the next stop. I have a sleep, and DREAM about gangsters. In Paris,

I don't book hotel just in case! But go straight to the address on the Ille De Cite deliver the painting, and get paid some money. No more problems. The rest of time was mine. Time for more practice. I knew that is what Harry meant. "Stay a few days. Enjoy yourself". I had some lunch at the café in the Pompidou Museum. I'd been there before, and I loved the museum for it's honesty. A lot of the workings of the museum, cables, pipes, are put on the outside, clear to see. If only, I thought, I could be more open, like that. In the café, I got to know some young students. They are from Denmark, Interior Design students in Copenhagen. We have a lot in common. During the Easter Break, they are studying English, in Bournemouth, and having a long weekend in Paris. With my increasing bravura, I get friendly with one lovely girl. I join the group for the rest of the day, seeing Paris, and spend the night in the girl's hotel room. DREAMS

Spend next day with the Danish group. See Paris by boat on Seine, visit art museums, see the film, 'Jules et Jim'. Another night with girl. Right not to book a hotel. She gives me her address in Denmark. Next morning, they all return to Bournemouth. We leave at The Place De Concorde, by the statues. I say goodbye to the girl. It was painful and sad.
It is a coincidence that it was here, in the film,' An American In Paris', that Gene Kelly danced that romantic fantasy ballet, to George Gershwin's great music. Inside me, now, I can feel those glorious colours, evocative of the changing moods of love; and feeling some of the same pain of lost love, as in the film.

On my own again, I tread water, to stay afloat. Lost and unsure after the Danish girl. I go into the Tuileries Gardens, sit down near the Louvre. #Bright Light; Dark MUSIC / DAYDREAM Images of aloneness, lost, doubts prey on me. Ice, cold, fear, snakes, the march of devil types, chopin death march. One Cobra snake, slimy, dripping, grows larger with an enormous mouth; eating people! Menacing image, Not living and risking. I hit an iceberg. See the headlines. "Going down." The old familiar down feelings. The last few days had seen tremendous bravery. Now it felt like a simulation. At least my daydreaming was rich, intense, not dull. Much work still to be done. I remember Harry. "Small steps, keep practicing". Harry seems close. Feel lifted as result. The Spring sunshine, bathes and relaxes, like a warm bath robe.

I get a temporary job in the Tuilleries café. Cleaning and kitchen work. I have been there before with a friend, last year. I get friendly with one of waitresses, a student. We meet up for our lunch break and walk in the gardens and chat. I feel more assured It began to rain, and we went in the café for shelter. It was like a scene from a Trauffot film. All chatter, gestures, and touching hands. We exchanged contacts. After work, I got a hotel room. We met up in the evening and spent the night together in my hotel.

Friends of the café owner had a yacht moored at St. Jeanet on Cap Ferrat in the South of France. They were sailing in 10 days time around the Eastern Med., and needed extra hands. I had to go back to London to report to Harry, and said I would let them know. I met Harry, as arranged, Danny was there too, and I reported on my trip. They were very pleased. They gave me the encouragement to work on the yacht A few days later days, after a couple more meetings with Harry, I was on my way to the Cote D'Azur, by way of the Hi speed TVG Railway.

The guests on the yacht were an Arty lot. A French Cabaret Singer, an Italian artist, an American screenwriter, a documentary film maker, who was shooting material for a program about the European Aristocracy set. There were some girl friends and wives and there were also 2 or 3 musicians, guitarists. They were using the ship's studio to record some stuff for a C.D. They specialised in Gypsy guitar music, which comes under the heading of World Music. After an evening stint in the galley, I was ready for sleep.

Dreamed. I live, work with a Circle of creative, arty friends; some live together in art commune in the same block / art centre, like Tomato (like play / musical for my Pets Project. See under Plays. Some famous historical genius's live with us or visit. Bohemian atmosphere. American in Paris, romances, rows, fights, rehearsals, Art shows, concerts, recordings, plays. I do multi media [m /m] shows, with people like Laurie Anderson.

Dream I do multi media shows all over Europe. open air in Verona, Cesearea, Venice St Mark's square. I dream, do shows in the sky on clouds. See queues coming up from earth. It rains up and down, snow, fog hides the audience. Some of audience down below on hills. Sea, storms, lightning, show goes on people die in storm. Some of themes in m/m shows: politics, intrigue, espionage, mafia, conspiracies, Biltmore theory, capitalism v. fair world trade, terrorism, ecology. U.S. proposed expense sending men to Mars. U.K. expense on Iraq war. Film, T.V. of shows. Interviews. All this was daydreams and night dreams.

Awake, at daylight, I leave the boat in Majorca. Had enough. Didn't make it with any women on the cruise. Mojo up and down, hovering. In Palma I get hotel job, cleaning. Go to hotel gym for tone up.
Chance meeting in hotel bar, this bloke, a hotel guest, offers me a rep job in import / export of Ethnic Textiles based in Tunisia. Sales not my thing. Boring. Meet trekking group. They are performing some world music, with dancing, in the main square of Palma. Join with them. We go to the Sahara. Share food with Nomad Tribes. In Egypt, my group explore burial chambers. I fall asleep by Pyramids.

#Hi Fly Triumphal Music / DREAM: I'm down in big burial chamber. Sun hits gold throne thro crack in walls. Sends me floating up on this beam of gold light, thro. crack out into space. To a planet. Live with community of civilized humans. Kind people. I am cared for; feel loved; feel I belong, like Danny and Harry told me. I'm a stranger, yet, I'm taken in; no questions. Spend some months there. Women liberated; unconditional love. My hidden, repressed leadership qualities are exposed to daylight. Returning to Earth on a green light beam; which is really me feeling a little more harmony. But on the way attacked by ferocious team of angry, hungry tigers. They grow larger, then merge into one gigantic dragon like creature, spitting poison and acid. Sweating, shouting and in terror I throw myself sideways to escape......and wake up in the sand. In the shadow of the Pyramid, I feel slightly less bottled.

But, there is still more rising up. I want to be sick with it all. Emotionally. All this crap wants to come out. Volcano like. It must! Instinctively, when I get back to London, from Egypt, I head straight for Speakers Corner, and start shouting. I don't care if anyone listens. I am getting it out. I go on about corruption, injustice in politics. Wasting public money, killing the planet due to greed, and so on. I get quite a few claps, and cheers, apart from the jeers. I must be getting somewhere! [END]

[In the story, the music at each stage gets louder. Music of country I am in, or same piece. Story, writing starts shaky, longwinded. Gets tighter as I get more worldly, confident. Writing style to reflect change. Staccatto, lyrical passages to express different situations, moods]

'LONG DISTANCE TO GOD'

Characters: God, Anita, Hetty, Sue, Esther, Michael, Narrator

Scene: A Social Club

* Song: Printed copies.
* Sound effects Table
* CD Player

[Tikkun: To improve, repair]

Hetty: Big welcome and thanks to the Volunteer ladies from Tikkun Charity!

Michael: Have they come to teach us?

Anita: No. They are doing a Mitzvah; it's a kind service. And it gets them out the house.

Michael: Why is there so much Jewish study and learning? I thought you just love God, keep the Ten Commandments, and that's it.

Hetty: Well, when you love someone, you want to know all you possibly can about them, don't you. It's like that.

Michael: Oh, but why so many different types and branches of
          Jewish study? I mean, you can read:

[Do as a song]

          The Kabbalah and The Torah
          While the Chassids dance the Horah
          Study Talmud and the Mishna
          While the Tikkun do their Mitzvah
          There's theology, kiddology
          Aisha, Kasher and the Mystics
          There's Liberal and Progressive who are almost Roman
          Catholics
          Transdenominational and Jewish Renewal

          Pantheism, monoism are things that you'll......learn.
          Orthodox are poor and the Liberals usually rich
          If you want a bit of both of them, then join the Lubavitch!

          There's so many things to study
          It makes the study waters muddy.
          Just choose the branch which you prefers
          But if you want to be with ALL things Jewish,
          go along to Spurs!
          Hi!

[Phone rings. Michael answers it]

MICHAEL: Hello, Jewish Day Centre. Who is it?

God: God here. I heard you poking fun at Jewish studies; Let
          me tell you, don't knock it. As the focal point of it all, it's
          nice to feel wanted.

Hetty: God while you're there on the line, are you doing
          customer services today?

God: I don't usually, but I got an angel on holiday, so I'm covering. And this is the Soul Dept at customer services, by the way.

Hetty: Can I ask you this, oh all powerful, Omniscient Being. To you, how much is a penny?

God: To me, a penny is 1 million pounds.

Hetty: Oh All Knowing Being, to you, how long is a second?

God: To me a second is 1 million years.

Hetty: Oh Lord, give me a penny.

God: Just a second.

ESTHER: Can I ask you this, on behalf of a friend who has passed away. He didn't like to complain to you, so he has sent me an email. He says, "I got to the Pearly Gates and The Lord greeted me with a plate of sandwiches. I said, "Oh Lord, On my way up, I passed a huge banquet going on, way down below me. Tables and tables full of wonderful food and drink; endless crowds of people were eating, drinking and singing. The place was a bit hot, red and fiery, but they were having great time. And I'm in Heaven, and I only get a sandwich. Lord, why?" And The Lord replied, "Well, it's not worth cooking just for the two of us!"

GOD: Your friend should complain to the Restaurant at Customer Service.

Anita: Bie mir bistu shoene, my hubbie's playing away again.

God: You want the Relate Dept.

Sue: Can you give me a decision on this? My husband has
           also been playing around. Is that to do with the soul?

GOD: Maybe; go on, what happened!

Sue: Last year, my husband was in bed with the another
           woman, an orthodox, and, by mistake, said the wrong
           Blessing for love making. He said the Blessing for Root
           Vegetables. The woman just gave birth to a healthy, 3
           lb Baby Carrot. She keeps it in the fridge. She wants
           to know, if she makes vegetable soup with it, will she
           be committing Infanticide?My husband has to help with
           maintenance. Right now it's costing him £7.50 a Kilo.
           Should I stay with him?

God: Mmmm. No, That's not soul stuff; that's the fruit and veg
           dept.

Hetty: Well, you know all those wise words and affirmations,
           like: "Think positive; whatever you want, you can get".
           So, what did I get; a nasty spot on my bottom! [*tuchas*]
           And I never even prayed, or asked for it.

God: That's a body complaint. I told you, I only deal with the
           soul. What is in people's hearts. You need Customer
           Services, Body Parts.

Sue: Here's another wise saying, "The moment I decide
           where I want to go, the world will make room for me."
           Well, I decided to go to the toilet room, and what did I
           get; constipation!

God: That's Body Parts again.

Anita: Okay, I got a bent car fender from some parking
           offender But I didn't ask for it or make a request, so it's
           hard to digest. It's a brand new car, and.......

God: .... that's not my dept, little girl. That could be Body Parts again, or Divine Traffic and Highways. Complain to them. I'm above all that. Remember, you're talking to the great Hashem.

Hetty: But why do we all have the good and the bad, everyday, side by side? I thought two opposites couldn't exist in the same space, at the same time.

God: Hey, don't blind me with science. I still don't understand the 57 varieties of Heinz!

Anita: It's really not that simple to get the things you want, as those so called wise men and affirmations say.

God: Yes, I know; here's another one; "If I can conceive and believe, I can achieve."

Sue: And this one; "You can make your dreams reality." They make me sick! I like walking to get fit; saves on Gym fees. But what do I get? Painful knees!

God: Well pain is good for the soul. So you got bad legs; It will help take down your Ego a peg or two. Ha, ha?

Hetty: I got food allergies from eggs, cheese and E- Numbers. But no allergy from the food I hate, cucumbers!

God: That's the Angelic Food Dept., Complaints. I don't do the salad bowl; just food for the soul.

Sue: This one gets me: "I don't have to look for proof. Every day is a succession of small miracles." But a friend of mine is very ill. And yet he is into positive thinking. What's going on?

Anita: Here's another affirmation; "The only thing I expect today is another opportunity to live the best life I can." But I know a lady who is expecting, even though she's on the pill.

Hetty: How about this; "There are no limitations to the self, except those you believe in'." Yes, well I like de-stoned olives, but I find the one with a stone, which breaks an expensive gold crown that I just spent lot of money on, having repaired; Plus, I just cancelled my dental insurance. Life just ain't fair!

God: Yeah, well you got me there. With all the cruelty and injustice around, you just can't please.

Sue: For a lark, a friend and his mates Went on the mile long Southend Pier. They tried to look cool, but there are no dam toilets, And my friend got diarrhoea!

God: That's either Body Parts again, or civic buildings dept.

Hetty: I was making a dinner for important guests, but I'd run out of Miso for the soup......

God: No chicken stock?

Hetty: No, it has to be Miso. My husband is Japanese. We're the only Buddhist / Orthodox family, who eats Kosher Suishi. So I run to the local shop, but it's raining; I feel a hole in my waterproof shoe; the shop is shut, I do my nut; I don't like to complain, but now my best nylons have a stain.

God: Complain to Weather Dept. on that one, not me. Got to go now. And this not a free call, despite free will. You'll be getting a bill.

ANITA: Oh! Well....er....thanks for solving all of our problems!

GOD: My pleasure.

Sue: My friends here, we got some jokes; Want to hear some?

God: Go on; slay me.

Anita: "Doctor, I can't pronounce my F's, T's and H's". The doctor Well, you can't say fairer than that then.

Sue: Man went in with piece of lettuce sticking out of his touchas. Doctor says, "Mmm, that's strange". The Man says, "Yes, and that's just the tip of the Iceberg!"

Hetty: A mate told me that last year he gave his wife a special birthday present. A silver and fur lined coffin. This year his wife asks him, "You didn't get me a birthday present?" He says, "No. You haven't used the one from last yearyet!".

Anita: One freezing cold night, there was a knock on the front door. My Mother in Law was standing on the front step. She says, "Can I stay here tonight?" I shouted, "Yes", and slammed the door.

God: Ha, ha. Yes, well, I heard them all before. Boy, this is some Mitzvah you Tikkun ladies are doing! Listen, I've helped you, now you can do a small job for Me.

Hetty: Small...how small?

God: Small in terms of the never ending space time continuum of eternity and the Universe, but huge in terms of making the World a better place to live in.

[Sound - noise with instruments, and
shouts of hallelujah - 5 seconds]

HETTY: Wow, THAT big!

Anita: Wouldn't you be better at a job like that? Why us?

God: I can't do it. People wouldn't believe me. I'm different. I'm bigger. I'd scare people. It's got to come from ordinary folk like you. I've heard your complaints, and you are the same as all the rest, so they will listen to you. And you're Tikun ladies So everyone will respect what you say. Plus, your names will go down in history.

Anita: Go down; you mean, 'down', like 'falling' in love? Listen.

[Sound effect - falling - thud]

God: No, I mean, you'll be famous

Hetty: Like, 'I'm a Celebrity…. get me out of here'?

GOD: Bigger.

Anita: Like Sheryl Cole?

God: Bigger.

SUE: Nelson?

God: Bigger. More famous

SUE: Will we be deaded?

GOD: You will be if you don't shut up! Enough! Here is what you do. This phone line you're talking to me on will turn into a road. It's a long uphill walk, but will seem short. Slay the monster guarding the way; if not, go around it; use the By - Pass road. At the end of the road, you'll be high, high above the Earth. A strong iron gate guards the secret platform there. It can only be opened by Love and faith; if not... use the key!

GOD: Take these loudspeakers, amplifiers and microphones, and plug them into the phone line on the platform. Here's the script you're to read out. It's an announcement to the world about a new World Wide Lottery I'm starting. It will be heard live, by everyone across the world, and on telephones and mobiles. It's also a peace ultimatum to the world.

HETTY: Sounds like Blackmail; or match fixing!

GOD: Can't be helped; people have tried everything else; this is last throw of the Dice; last chance saloon. I must intervene.

ANITA: I can't go. I can't stand heights. And I got a cold;

GOD: Listen, This is the best medicine; helping mankind; it will get your endorphines racing around. Everybody would feel a lot better if they spread more positive vibes and had more laughs; it's the best medicine. And, I can make you go, you know. I have plenty of dirt I can dish on you. Oh yes!

HETTY: Oh, more blackmail.

GOD: I told you; it's the last ditch trump card. It has to be played.

ANITA: Why?

GOD: Because people are so difficult. Here, take this trowel.

SUE: What's it for?

GOD: To spread the word. Let's sing……

[Song: Tune: 'Aint She Sweet']

ALL: Aint it mad
          The way that people are so bad
          So I ask you very confidentially
          Aint they mad

          We've had enough
          Of this war and killing stuff
          Now I tell you very controversially
          That's enough

          We need some love
          That is our purpose
          From heaven above
          If you will help us

          One last chance
          To get the world to sing and dance
          Now I'll give you inside information
          It's one last chance

HETTY: And after we've done this job?

GOD: I'll send a thank you email.

SUE: Any reward?

GOD: You'll be famous like I said. And I'll try and get you on
           'I'm a Celebrity'.

           [Sound Effect - walking - 5 seconds]

NARRATOR: *But this is only a 10 minute play. They got there on
           the Sabbath. But dilemma. To work on the Sabbath
           and incur God's Wrath, or do this job for God and
           incur His pleasure. The thought of being on 'I'm a
           Celebrity…. get me out of here' won the day.*

*ALL FOUR WOMEN: Make sound of talking together for few
           seconds.*

NARRATOR: *They arrive at the gate.*

HETTY: He said Love and faith open the gate; better use
           the key!

NARRATOR: *Then, on the phone line platform, they set up the
           Sound equipment.*

           [Sound effect - setting up equipment - 5 seconds]

SUE: Testing, testing……

NARRATOR: *And so, on the telephone line platform, high above
           The Earth, they read the message to the listening
           world.*

ANITA: "God has asked us to make this announcement to all of
         you In the world on His behalf, because we're humans
         like all of you, and I guess we look pretty in dresses…..do
         you like them? I got this one from John Lewis….in a sale;
         and the shoes are from……..Oh, sorry."

SUE: Why does small talk always take so long!

HETTY: To all you listening in the streets, your office, on your phones, these words come direct from the mouth of The Lord. "Yea, verily I say unto you, and it shall come to pass........ I, The Lord God, am starting a Universal Lottery, and you'll all be winners "Everyone of you will win, and the prize money will be credited to your own special Lottery account. And it will be means tested according to your income. No tickets, no cost, free; but there is a price. You have all got to get along; no more squabbles and wars. Yes, and I'll close the account of anyone causing trouble".

ANITA: Oh no, listen. There's trouble already.

          [Sound effect - noise of war, fighting - 15 seconds]

GOD: Look at them. They are fighting again because of the means test. Some are getting more Lottery money than others. I played my card; I tried the Blackmail. Thanks for helping ladies...No fame; no TV show! You're right; go on with the study and learning; it's our best chance.

Anita: Thanks for coming today Tikkun ladies. JAMI has a full program of activities and guests. We had David Kossoff here once. He gave a talk. He made a film, 'Kid 4 2 Farthings'. A low budget production which I always felt short changed the audience.

          And it's for a good end; not for my profit help recovery of sick.... and politicians. Well, I'm still alive.

          Yes, that's right, I see no end of kids dying around world No, there aint no justice here for man... Or the Holocaust, and the lives it cost.

God: Like I say, free will; it's up to each one of you.

Michael: I get more things of no use, than what I ask for. Who sends this crap?

God: Watch it ...., you're on the border line.

Michael: But if you're the All Powerful, Omniscient Being, etc, how come you don't cut out the bad stuff?

God: Oh no, that's because of free will. For me to interfere would be disastrous. Life's a lottery; you win, some you lose........ And then you all think, "What comes after us?"

NB: *Usually a long hard rocky road to peace but this only 10 min. play; so condense Not a short road. Took days. Faulty Sat Nav. And stop the spending on defence; close the Arms factories.*

12.02.13

MODERN PURIM STORY

Title: **'From Pain to Champagne'.**

Main characters:

Producer

Arnold:	[King Azeheraus, non Jew]	Head of TV Production
Hal:	[Haman, villain, non Jew]	Production Assistant
Vera:	[Queen Vashti, non Jew]	Top show presenter
Esther:	[Queen Esther, heroine, Jew]	New show presenter
Mo:	[Mordechai, hero, Jew]	Head scriptwriter.

This version of the Purim story, is set, not in ancient Persia, but in a modern country; Los Angeles, America. And not in in the palace of a King, but in the offices and studio of a TV Production company. But the story is similar; the lessons much the same; How a good race of people survived against hatred.

The scene; *the offices of a modern TV Production company, Pan T.V. Productions. A row is going on between the TV company Producer Abe [King Azeheraus], the star presenter of their TV show, Vera [Queen Vashti] and Hal [Haman] the assistant Producer.*

Opening music

Narrator: *The Purim Spiel; a musical play.*

Producer What the hell do you mean, you won't do it! Won't do it?
Arnold You're under contract sister!

Vera Listen, wise guy, read that contract clause; "Nothing
Immoral, indecent or racial!

Producer But all we want you to do is the number in a bathing
Arnold suit; nothing more; you can use a one piece if you want.
But the song is about holidays, the sea, sunbathing, and
all that... what's so terrible?

Vera I told you before, it will affect my standing, my clean
profile in the business.......sorry to leave you all at sea,
and all that!

Hal I told you that clause would back fire on us; but you
wouldn't listen; you was so stuck on her......

Producer Shut up! You're holding out for more money aren't you?
Arnold Lead presenter, singer on the show; You already earn
more than me!

Vera It's not money. I just won't do stuff that could jeopardize
my career; I'm the Julie Andrews of TV presenting.

Arnold You weren't so fussy about your morals when I first
met you!

Vera That was for my career; and this is for my career. I gotta
keep a clean image for this kind of work.

Arnold: But I told you, we've got to do some specials to boost our audience ratings. You know the other TV company, Meridian, is starting to head us; doing this racy, controversial stuff; we got to up the tempo.

Hal   She turned down their offer to switch to them.

Vera   Yeah, and my agent agreed. Stick with you for the clean image he said; if I wanted a saucy image, I'd be better off with Meridian; money wise, for sure.

Arnold   If it wasn't that we need to boost our ratings with some special draws on the show, I wouldn't need to ask you. None of the others on the team has your attraction; you're the pull!

Vera   Yeah, I carry the show, and I won't do this!

Producer: Okay, get out. You're fired. I'll find someone even better!
Arnold

Narrator: After Vera leaves, the TV company holds auditions for a new female star presenter.

Cast Director: We have to find a replacement for Vera, today! Rehearsals for the next show start this week. You, the audience will help us decide. Let us know who you think is the best. As usual, our presenters have to be multi talented. So first we'll try you all at reading, and then Singing. So first you will each read out a Limerick and a Tongue Twister to test your reading skills.

Narrator: Producer Arnold holds auditions for a new female presenter for his TV show. Three girls wait their turn to audition, before an invited audience.

Abe: As usual, our new presenters have to be good news readers and fast. To test your skills, in turn, you will each read out some Limericks and Tongue Twisters. The audience will decide the best.

Narrator The first girl auditions

1ˢᵗ Girl A flea and a fly in a flue,
Were trapped and knew not what to do,
Said the fly, 'Let us flee'
'Let us fly', said the flea,
So they flew through a flaw in the flue.

There's a train at 4.04," said Miss Jenny, Four tickets I'll take - have you any?" Said the man at the door, "Not four for 4.04, For four for 4.04 are too many."

There was a young lady of Perkins, Who was exceedingly fond of green gerkins; She ate a whole quart, Which was more than she ought, For it pickled her internal workin's.

If a noisy noise annoys an onion, an annoying noisy noise annoys an onion more!

Surely Shirley shall sell Sheila's seashells by the seashore.

Which witch wishes to switch a witch wristwatch for a Swiss wristwatch?

The butter Betty Botter bought could make her batter bitter, so she thought she'd better buy some better butter!

She sells sea-shells on the sea-shore. The shells she sells are sea-shells, I'm sure. For if she sells sea-shells on the sea-shoreThen I'm sure she sells sea-shore shells.

2ⁿᵈ girl   I'd rather have fingers than toes; I'd rather have ears than a nose, And as for my hair, I'm glad it's all there; I'll be awfully sad when it goes.

A tutor who tooted the flute, tried to teach two young tooters to toot; Said the two to the tutor: "Is it harder to toot, or To tutor two tooters to toot?"

There once was an old man of Lyme, Who married three wives at a time. When asked, "Why the third?" He said, "One's absurd, And bigamy, sir, is a crime."

Not many an anemone is enamoured of an enemy anemone.

Five fine Florida florists fried fresh flat flounder fish fillet.

A three-toed tree toad loved a two-toed he-toad that lived in a too-tall tree.

The skunk sat on a stump and thunk the stump stunk, but the stump thunk the skunk stunk.

Three Swedish switched witches watch; three Swiss Swatch watches" switches. Which Swedish switched witch watch which Swiss Swatch watch witch?

3ʳᵈ girl   There was an old woman took snuff, Who said she was happy enough, For she sneezed when she pleased, And was pleased when she sneezed, And that is enough about snuff.

The maid was a-bluster, around with a duster. Was really a-fluster a-dusting a bust. But when she had dusted, The bust it was busted.

A jolly young chemistry tough, while mixing a compounded stuff, Dropped a match in the vial, and after a while - They found his front teeth and one cuff.

Shep Schwab shopped at Scott's Schnapps shop. One shot of Scott's Schnapps stopped Schwab's watch.

Top chopstick shops stock top chopsticks......and........ If A Dog Chews Shoes, What Shoes Should He Choose To Chew.

Red rubber baby buggy bumpers bounce.

How much wood would a woodchuck chuck if a woodchuck could chuck wood?

Whether the weather be cold or whether the weather be hot. Whatever the weather we'll weather the weather, Whether we like it or not.

Narrator: At the end of the reading auditions…….

Cast Director: *[To audience]* Vote now for the best and fastest reader?

Narrator: Audience votes with hand held keypads

Cast Director: Esther wins the reading audition!. Now the singing auditions

Narrator: The three girls do their singing auditions and audience votes. Songs to be selected.

Cast Director: Esther you won the singing and you are now our new lead presenter!

Esther: Oh thank you. I'm so happy. When do we start rehearsals?

Hal   We film the next show in two week's time. Rehearsals start at once.

Narrator   *Press conference. Photos. TV Co to throw evening party.*

Narrator: *The story continues*

Narrator   *Over lunch, Mo tells Hal the latest news about Meridian, their very successful rival TV Company*

Mo   Hal, in confidence, have you heard on the grapevine that Meridian, is considering / making a bid / take over bid for us?

Hal   Yeah, we heard; but Producer Arnold don't know yet. Glad you came to me first. I'll pass it on; don't you warn him. Better from me. But I'll make sure he knows it was you who broke the news. He'll be grateful it was you who warned him. Thanks buddy.

Narrator   *Hal doesn't mean this, and has no intention of telling Producer Abe about Mo. Oh no! He'll take the credit himself. He doesn' t like Mo. He's envious of his writing skills; and for that matter Hal doesn't like Jewish people, period. And television is full of them!*

Hal: Listen, we've chosen the subject for the 'Hot Topics'
            section of the next show; we'll be looking at minority
            groups again; yeah, we've done it before, but this
            time we'll be taking a look at the anti Minorities side,
            including the Jews. You know, the usual problems
            they bring; taking jobs, housing... that's the angle.
            Write me up the usual questions and answers........"

Mo: *[Mo knows how indispensible he is]* I will not! Your
            brainwave of course....still got that bee in your
            bonnet; no way!! Still jealous of the Jewish people!
            It's still eating you up. How long have we worked
            together? You're crazy! And you expect me to do the
            script!!

Hal   Listen, buddy, you're under contract! We need
            controversy. Something to hit the papers, the news.
            You've seen our viewing figures last month.

Mo   No way! It'll inflame a nation; upset half our audience.

Hal   It's risky, but this is how Meridian's audience figures
            are shooting up; doing the saucy songs, blue comedy
            and controversial political stories........ We've got to
            fight them at their......."

Mo   "........I know all that. But, hey, no way man. I won't
            be a part of that. You expect me to slag off my own
            people!

Narrator   *And that's basically how the racial trouble began. The
            story continues ....*

Mo   No! I don't get involved with this unethical
            monstrosity. Hey, mister, you know with my contract,
            you can't produce a show without my script.

Hal   You'll do it, and we can make you do it! If you don't back down, we'll get rid of all the Jews on the staff and replace them with non Jewish, old school, tie, public school friends of mine and Arnold's.

Narrator   *Pan TV Co board meeting. Mo not there. Executives only.*

Producer Arnold   Mo has a screwed down contract. He can refuse projects if and only if there are justifiable reasons. The 'get out clause'.

Co. Lawyer: Phil   The only way we can get Mo to change his mind is by making enforced redundancies of his Jewish pals on the staff. And it will be like death to Mo if he allows that to happen!

Arnold   That sounds like some kind of blackmail. But we don't have time to play around. We got another show coming up. And we got to get Esther up to speed.

Co Lawyer Phil   So you have details of the plan in front of you. The Plan is to plant incriminating evidence of criminal embezzlement in the accounts of the TV company, with forged proof of Jewish staff involvement. This is our legal justification for the Jewish staff redundancies. It's the lever to get Mo to change his mind; and go ahead and write the script for the next show about racialism in general and the Jewish problem in particular.

Arnold   Let's vote!

[Vote taken]

Arnold   Plan approved!

Narrator   *The board go on to discuss their TV company other plan to thwart Meridian TV threatening take over bid, by boosting their own ratings; by attracting higher audience figures with some. specials; saucy and politically controversial shows.*

Narrator   *Mo hears about the board meeting and the plan against the Jewish staff. Upset and down, Mo drinks in down town bar. A secretary at Pan TV Company, close to Esther, tells him more of the plan. Mo listens and tells her to tell Esther to plead with Producer to change his mind. Mo fed up off in more ways than one!*

Narrator   *Evening party to celebrate Esther's success. Mo doesn't go.*

Esther   *[To Producer Arnold sitting at party table with Hal and others]* This plan I've heard to get rid of all the Jews on your staff. You mustn't go ahead with it. Why I've never heard of such a thing. And I'm Jewish; does that include me?

Producer   No, no, of course not. And Esther dear, please don't
Arnold   interfere in things you nothing about. It's not your affair baby.

Esther   I implore you to save Mo and the rest of staff. I'm Jewish too remember.

Hal   We're not letting you go Esther! But the others go! And that's final.

Esther   And I heard you're planning to make Jewish staff redundant in other TV Companies. What about the racial laws The Law on racial equality? You could be in big trouble!

Hal   We got friends in high places.

Esther   You mean the Mob!

Hal   Keep out of it Esther

Esther   Please I beg you. I'll do a good job you'll see

Hal   We know you will.

Esther   But if you don't stop this terrible plan, God knows what I'll do!

Arnold   Don't get so upset Esther darling!

Esther   Well Arnold if you don't cancel your disgusting plan, I'll leave too! And by way, do you know it was Mo who advised you guys about Meridian's take over intentions! He is loyal to you and you are going to destroy him!!

Arnold   It was Hal who warned me about M.

Esther   No, no! It was Mo who warned Hal.

Arnold   Is this true Hal?

Hal   No way!

Arnold   I want the truth

Hal   Mo may have said something.

Arnold   So it's you who's stirring up the hate campaign against the Jews. You even wanted to throw out Jewish staff in other TV companies, like Meridian. You know what, because Mo may have saved us, I'm giving him promotion. He's shown loyalty. Hal throw Mo a party!

Narrator   Hal protests, cringes and squirms.

Arnold   *[Smoking cigar and putting arm round Esther]* You're out Hal. You've gone too far!. And you get no references, oh no! And you know what, we'll cut out the racialist part of the next show. That should satisfy Mo. I've see what's been going on round here and I've been a fool.

Esther   Thank you Arnold. Thank you!!

Arnold   I'll even update, improve the contracts and pay of all our Jewish staff. As for Meridian's expectations of take over bid for us, they can go take a hike! If Esther does the good job we expect......

Esther   ....I will, I will, you'll see. And I'll do the saucy and you can cover the political controversial..... but not racial.........

Arnold   ......Great!..........then that should boost our ratings and advertising revenue. And we can stick fingers up to Meridian!

Narrator   Hal goes to another party table where he has friends

Hal   You heard Mo is holding out, and refuses to write the shows.

Friends   All you can do is sack him. Mo will contest. Invoke the 'Get out clause' and fight over the "Justifiable reasons." What else is there!

Narrator *Back to Esther's table.*

Arnold   Keep out of my affairs Esther. We've just hired you. Count yourself lucky. Do your presenting job well, but don't try and muscle in or trick me. Here, now this is the boy we got lined up for a two bit part in the show.

Narrator *Male singer in brief bathing costume with chorus of singers / dancers does the song Vera refused to do and was fired for. This is the song about the sea, that Esther has to sing in a bathing suit in their next TV show, to increase audience ratings. The song is done here, with boy & girl chorus;*

By The Beautiful Sea

[In the film, "FOR ME AND MY GIRL" / Garland / Kelly

Might find a recording]
By the sea, by the sea, by the beautiful sea!
You and me, you and me, oh how happy we'll be!
When each wave comes a-rolling in
We will duck or swim,
And we'll float and fool around the water.
Over and under, and then up for air,
Pa is rich, Ma is rich, so now what do we care?
I love to be beside your side, beside the sea,
Beside the seaside, by the beautiful sea!

Party Guests and Audience sings
to tune: **'My Favourite Things'**
[Instrumental recording]

Vashti and Esther, old Mordechai and Haman
We've all grown up with our Festival of Purim
Short Winter days and the promise of Spring
That's when we remember this great Purim thing.

Dreidels and spin tops, ice cream and sweeties;
Cheese cake and sardines and other nice eaties.
Moses and boiled eggs, Menorahs, oil lamps
The fasting and prayers gives our legs the cramps.
Chicken soup mit Kreplach, and smelly fried fish balls;
Driving to the "Dodgers", after prayers in the Shaul.
Mother's tears of pride, on her son's Barmitzvah;
Then her tears of distress, when he marries a Shiksa.

Cast with audience. Sing to tune: **I DREAMED A DREAM**
[Brass Band Recording]

Why can't we work for peace on Earth,
If we can think of peace in Heaven?
Ah, Peace, just what would it be worth.
Imagine no more nine eleven.

And if all countries cut Defence,
They could afford to pay off their debts.
Will they talk peace, climb off the fence?
What are the odds, what are the bets?

[Middle 8 Bridge]

Within our hearts there is no land.
There is no colour, race or creed.
Just to be a happy band.
A happy peace is what we ne......ed, ...what we need.

Come on, and get your act together.
Life is too short for wasting time.
Some is an Ego act, my brother. Our leaders, yours and mine.

Don't waste your lives on greed and rage.
Just try to simply empathise.

The lights are up, we're on the stage.
Stop churning out your stupid lies.

The Middle East is up in flames.
Israel still fights for freedom too.
So many lives, so many names.
And they want peace, like me and you…..
……like me and you.

16.11.13

'MIRACLE ON
WOLSKA STREET'

[Modern version of the Chanukah Story]

Run time of the play: about 15 minutes. Run time plus the karaoke party, and the Fashion Show: about 45 minutes.

Characters: Staff at Mannies ladies wear: **Mannie, Sarah, Hannah** * 2 x Narrators * Police * Polish M.P. * European member * Rabbi * Pope * Landlord * Home workers: **Esther, Rebecca. Jakob of Finklesteins**

* FX: Sound effects director. [Sound effects by: http://www.freesfx. co.uk]
* Karaoke / party director.
* Fashion Show director.

Scene:
A Jewish dress company, Mannies Ladies Wear, on Wolska Street, Warsaw, January, 1936.

1st Narrator:
You know, there are miracles and there are miracles. Here is the story of a real one. It echoes the original Chanukah story, when a small, defenceless people survive and beat a huge powerful force. That's what we call a miracle.

FX: Track 1: Background Music plays under narration - 32 secs

1st Narrator:
Mannies Ladies Wear, a smallish family business of a factory and shop, along with several other Jewish clothing companies, was going out of business. Their orders were being hijacked by Cosmo a large, rival, non Jewish clothing Company.

2nd Narrator:
In their bank account, just their last 10 Zloty of money. They had no dress orders, and were being victimised and pressured by Cosmo.

1st Narrator:
Cosmo had made several hostile take over bids, but so far, Mannies, had refused. It was their family business.

2nd Narrator:
Cosmo employed industrial espionage, stealing Mannies dress designs. Now Cosmo began using stronger tactics.

FX: Track 2: Window crash - 3 secs

Sarah:
"Oh no! God, what's that? There's a note."

Mannie:
[He reads note] "It will go on till you give in". Oy, Sarah, what can we do? Cosmo have the police in their pockets.

Sarah:
Yeah; it's hush money and huge bribes. The judges and politicians too.

Mannie: Why do they hate us? What have we done? This is not just business. It's not just about a dress making business, and making clothes. They've got the needle. They want to stitch us up.

FX: Track 19: SONG: Tune: **'My Favourite Things'.** Only 1st two verses - [Instrumental recording]

Mannie, Sarah, Hannah sing:

"They got the needle to all Jewish people.

They only see us
Through dark tinted spectacles.
Why are they broygas; is it because,
We have some talents they can only dream of.

Oy gevalt, I recall,
It'll take a miracle.
They want to break us;
It's getting disastrous.
They want to stitch us
These cruel sons of bitches.
They think they've got the whole thing sewn right up."

FX: Track 3: Transition Music - 5 secs

2nd Narrator:
The Cosmo threats and attacks go on: Mannie is not the only Jewish clothing company under the cosh; other businesses are targeted. A gang of thugs is employed by Cosmo and other non Jewish dress companies. Mannie's machinery is damaged.

FX: Track 2: Window smashed - 3 secs
FX: Track 4: Explosions in Mannie's factory - 10 secs
FX: Track 5: Phone dial to police - 6 secs

Police:
Yes?

Sarah:
Police, we have been attacked again.

Police:
We'll come right over.

FX: Track 3: Transition music - 5 secs
FX: Track 6: Police siren - 15 secs
FX: Track 7: Police Helicopter - 9 secs
FX: Track 8: Knock on door - 2 secs

Police:
We can't do anything. There's no proof.

Hannah:
We'll go to the Polish newspapers and the British press and radio; they will help us. We'll print protest leaflets; Shimon, our friend, the printer will help.

FX: Track 3: Transition music - 5 secs
FX: Track 9: Radio sounds - 11 secs

1st Narrator
[Imitates Radio News reader. Posh voice]
This is the BBC World Service. A number of racial attacks are reported in Warsaw. We've been asked to help. Well, just stop it, you naughty boys! Other more pleasant news.......Roosevelt re - elected; Hitler, that naughty boy, invades Rhineland; Abyssinia War; Spanish Civil War, though it doesn't sound very civil; Olympic Games in Berlin, that naughty boy Hitler again, has got upset when he loses; Edward 8th abdicates, and Mrs Simpson divorces from British husband, not American, as thought, and cites misconduct at Hotel de Paris in Maidenhead; the town is well named. Mrs Simpson, may di - vorce be with you.........

FX: Track 9: Radio sounds - 11 secs
FX: Track 10: Printing machine - 15 secs

1st Narrator:
The leaflets are printed, for free, and distributed to the press and media.

FX: Track 3: Transition music - 5 secs

2nd Narrator:
Back in the factory office.

Sarah:
And we'll get a petition with the other struggling Jewish garment companies to our government and to the European Court of Racial Equality.

Hannah:
Here are the petition names: There's Goldbloom, Schmaltz, Oy Vey, large sizes, Finklestein Teen Wear, Gerbshaft Alterations, Pinkus, Oy, Let It Out, Pimplebums………..

Mannie;
Wait…… it's no use, I'll have to get a pen and write them all down!

FX: Track 3: Transition music - 5 secs

2nd Narrator:
A meeting of the Polish government.

FX: Track 11: Pig noise - 4 secs
FX: Track 12: Donkey - 7 secs

1st Narrator;
An Polish M.P. speaks in the debate.

Polish M.P:
We have Mannie's petition, but the government can't help; we can't interfere in private affairs. Now, we've urgent business. We must get on and pass this bill to increase our salaries, and cut public spending.

1st Narrator:
To a meeting of the European Court of Racial Equality: also bribed.

FX: Track 13: Chimps - 5 secs

European M.P:
Any important business? No……. LUNCH!!

FX: Track 3: Transition music - 5 secs

2nd Narrator:
They visit Rabbi for advice:

Rabbi:
Give in; merge with Cosmo. Look what you'll save in overheads!

FX: Track 14: Phone ring - 11 secs

Mannie:
Hello, is that Rome, 2645718?

Vatican:
Vatican. Yes?

Mannie;
Vatican? Sorry, wrong number.

FX: Track 14: Phone ring - 11 secs

Mannie:
Hello, Pope? *[Sneezes]* Atishoo!

Pope:
Ah, bless you.

Mannie:
Can you help us?

Pope:
[Camp voice] Oh, the Jewish question again! My advice; convert. I
did; I used to be straight; now look at me! But I'll help; make me a
long robe in pink darlings!

FX: Track 3: Transition music - 5 secs

1st Narrator;
Mannie, and staff, disheartened, have an office meeting.

FX: Track 14; Phone ring - 11 secs

2nd Narrator:
It's the owner and landlord of Mannie's factory and shop.

Landlord:
Mannie, you're behind with your rent. I shall be forced to distrain
upon your machinery.

Mannie:
You filthy swine!

1st Narrator;
The meeting continues.

Sarah:
Okay, we agree. The bank will give us a loan when they see our order book full. So, we start work on our new Spring Collection. It must be ready in two weeks; we have a place in the Warsaw Fashion Show in February.

Hannah:
Cosmo mustn't know, so we can't do the work here in the factory; we farm the work out, in secret, to our loyal home workers and friends.

Mannie:
With just 10 Zloty left in our account, it will take a miracle. One thing helps, Spring Collections are cheaper to make; use less material.

FX: Track 3: Transition music - 5 secs

2nd Narrator:
Boys secretly take the new dress designs to the home workers under cover of newspaper rounds. They go on bicycles.

FX: Track 15: Motor Bike - 11 secs

1st Narrator:
The dressmaking, stitching and sewing begins.

FX: Track 16: Drills - 14 secs
FX: Track 17: Chainsaw - 12 secs
FX: Track 18: Tension build up & uplift music - 32 secs

1st Narrator:
The Home workers work day and night. It's all hands to the wheel. They have two weeks to finish the Collection. Two weeks before the Fashion Show. Let's listen to the women stitching, chatting and singing, as they work at home

Esther:
You know our butcher Kossoff is complaining he can't get hold of his usual meat quota. It's been cut by 25 %, and no reason given. At the Bani Brith meeting last Monday, you were there, Mrs. Pinbloom said she was buying more vegetables and fruit for the family, and saving on meat anyway.

Rebecca:
I know, yes. My cousin, Schnabel, you know the doctor, he's into nutrition, And he gave a talk about food, and how we can still get goodness from more vegetables and fish and herring; he sent me the transcript.

Esther:
If the business goes on like this, and Mannie looking so sad, we are all cutting back on food anyway. This new Collection is the last chance saloon for us and Mannie.......

FX: Track 20: Sunrise, Sunset - 90 secs. Play ONLY first 2 x verses, and first 2 x choruses:
[Instrumental recording]

Esther: Verse 1:

How does this happen to our business?
What kind of creeps can be so cruel?
One day they'll get their own come uppance. I pray in Shaul.

Rebecca: Verse 2:

How are Matilda and her sister?
Will their landlord put up the rent?
Mostly bad news, except just one that's
Heaven sent.

Esther: Chorus 1:

My boy, your girl
Are in a whirl;
They get on so well.

Now we should think about the wedding.
It'll lift us from this living hell.

Rebecca: Chorus 2:

We must not wait.
Who knows our fate.
Daily threats once more.
All we can do is stick together,
And watch for a knocking at the door.

2nd Narrator:
Jakob, owner of Finklestein Teen Wear, comes in.

Jakob;
So, how's it going Mannie?

Mannie:
I think we'll do it. How, don't ask. For two weeks, no cash flow, but the Collection is nearly ready.

FX: Track 14: Phone ring - 11 secs

Hannah:
There, the Collection is ready!!

FX: Track 3: Transition music - 5 secs

1st Narrator:
Mannies and all staff throw a celebration party for their wonder achievement.

Jakob:
Tell me how you did it Mannie?

Mannie:
Well, we're sworn to secrecy; and now you too. I'll tell only you, as my very best friend; and now that yours, and the other Jewish businesses are saved. We had an 'angel'. No, not from up there; it was a wealthy, old customer; she gave us the money, and helped save the rest of you too.

Sarah:
Keep schtoom Jakob. We're letting everyone believe it was The Lord. And it's good publicity for the business......

Hannah:
And it's giving everyone a huge lift, an inspiration. Okay, we survived once again. We won this battle, but not the War ahead.

Mannie:
Now, let's celebrate. And everyone, this reminds us, what amazing, inspiring people we humans can be sometimes.

FX: Track 19: Tune:' My Favourite Things' - 4. 20 minutes. Play the whole track [[Instrumental recording]

Mannie, Hannah, Sarah sing:

They've got the needle,
But usually, they forget,
They are the ones who need all
The help they can get.
We and our brains are at work hand in hand.
You see brains like this in that Russell Brand.

From Haifa to New York
In arms and computers.
From mobile and science
And finance really suits us.
Show business runs in the brains of us lot.
Who do you think wrote this Chanukah plot.

[This song plays on. Now, Hasidic type dancing; guests join in]

Then: Member's / Staff Talent Party / Karaoke, and FX music, etc.

Then: Warsaw Fashion Show; Members / Staff on Catwalk

FX: Catwalk Music

Mannie:
Now we'll get the bank loan. We got the orders coming in. ....

All:
A miracle. Muzeltov!

FX: SONG: Tune: **'I DREAMED A DREAM'**. *The instrumental Brass Band version which I have. Lyrics: Same as ones in the Purim Play:*

Why can't we work for peace on Earth,
If we can think of peace in Heaven?
Ah, Peace, just what would it be worth.
Imagine no more nine eleven.

And if all countries cut Defence,
They could afford to pay off their debts.
Will they talk peace, climb off the fence?
What are the odds, what are the bets?

[Middle 8 Bridge]

Within our hearts there is no land.
There is no colour, race or creed.
Just to be a happy band.
A happy peace is what we ne…...ed, ……..what we need.

Come on, and get your act together.
Life is too short for wasting time.
Some is an Ego act, my brother.
Our leaders, yours and mine.

Don't waste your lives on greed and rage.
Just try to simply empathise.
The lights are up, we're on the stage.
Stop churning out your stupid lies.

The Middle East is up in flames.
Israel still fights for freedom too.
So many lives, so many names.
And they want peace, like me and you…..
……like me and you.

PLAY TITLE: *"JUST OUTSIDE BERLIN"* 04.03.09

Characters:

Bill, Concert Tour Manager * Matt, Press Officer for Peace Talks * Martin, Press Officer for Concert Tour * Marx Brothers * Announcer * Mickey Rooney * Fred Astaire * Cole Porter * 1st & 2nd Senators * Judy Garland * Groucho Marx * Phil, Pathe Newsman * Oscar Levant

Characters in Dream:

Judy Garland * Plato * Oscar Wilde * Descartes * Woody Allen Richard Wagner * Goethe * Beethoven * Leonardo Da Vinci John Lennon * Answerous (Fabled Creature) The Paralyser (Monster)

Scenery, Props:
Back Projections, i.e. Chagall; scenery of countries, towns of the celebrities Judy interviews. Music, songs for each celebrity / country. Animation projections. Laser lighting can convey moods, emotions; Holograms.

SCENE:
Rehearsal Hall, Babelsberg Film Studios, Berlin suburb, June 1939. Huge hall. Stage, mikes. Long way, at far end, is Food and Drink corner. Rehearsals being recorded and filmed. Also scenes in Commissary and street

DIALOGUE:

Bill: Hi, everyone. Gather round. Just a few intros. Welcome. I'm Bill, Your Concert Tour Manager. This here is the famous Babelsberg Film Studios. Some classic German films are made here, like, The Blue Angel and Metropolis. We are given use of this huge Sound stage. We will be rehearsing the show here for the North European leg of the Tour. Hollywood, The U.S. Treasury and Sponsors, have put the Concert Tour together. These concerts are Part of the Goodwill Mission. You know the importance of this latest Goodwill Mission and Peace Talks. The aim, to build bridges and avoid war. Welcome today, to some Delegates and Ministers from The Senate, The House Of Commons, and The League Of Nations. They are here to watch some of the rehearsal. God speed To you all. Busby Berkeley, our show director, is taking today's first Rehearsals. A few words from Matt, the Press Officer for the Peace Talks Mission.

Matt: Just to remind you, that the German Foreign Minister has accepted our invitation to attend today's rehearsals. He should be here soon. Do chat to him, but use tact. This is the last year of the 30's decade. Let's hope we can be successful and help them see sense.

Bill: Now, the Press Officer for the Concert Tour. Martin.

Martin: As you know, we have invited the leaders of the German Government to our Berlin show. As yet, we have no reply. But, yes, do chat to the Minister and his aides when they come. We want to break down barriers. And most of you stars will be known to the Minister. It might help. You know the Germans will not allow the MGM Publicity Tour for The Wizard of Oz, to go ahead.

But it's good to go for the other European countries. So welcome to the stars who are giving of their time, freely, despite their heavy commitments. Let us hope our shows help The Mission. Okay, let's get it on the road. Good luck everyone.

Bill: Right. We have a lot to get through. Guests, enjoy the rehearsals, the food and drink. Make the Minister welcome. Remember what it's all for. First up, singing with the MGM Tour Orchestra is ....

[Suddenly, two of the Marx Brothers come in a window, playing Cards on an attached folding table. Harpo comes up through the Stage on an elevator, blowing his horn. Strings of doughnuts round his neck. He prances around the guests and stars, putting Doughnuts on their wrists. Chico plays the piano. Harpo joins him. They do their usual funny bits of business. Groucho tells some jokes]

Groucho: When do we get the Baseball scores? Can we get the New York Times? Get Lana Turner to wake me at 10. Coffee black Shirt, blue. By the time I'm finished with Lana, I will be black And blue! You can't mess with her. If I'm not in, don't wake me. And remember, on my tombstone I want, "Once, bone idle, now, bone idle forever"!

[More jokes and Marx Brothers business]

Announcer: Okay boys. That's your bit. But you know you are down for just ten minutes. Okay? Now, Judy please. Judy Garland everyone! And the MGM Tour Orchestra. (Applause)

[Judy starts singing, "Swing Mr. Charlie". Over this music The stars and delegates chat, in the corner of the hall, by The refreshments table]

Rooney: Judy, what a trouper. Always on the button. She's a delight But you know what demons she's got. She is writing poems now. Wistful stuff. Lost love and so on. This crush she has on Artie Shaw, will go nowhere. We are worried about her.

Astaire: She is too young for him. What is he, twenty years older?

Rooney: Yeah. And she's still in grief over losing her father. What is it, four years ago. Family blood love like that is rare. It's hard

Astaire: I heard she just got her first car from MGM. A thank you gift.

Rooney: She makes enough for them. She has all the love from her work. But she badly needs a man to fill in for her Dad. The right man. But I'm not the right one for her. I'm just a 'right one'! I'm too wild. Always looking around.

Astaire: Judy did a great job on the Wizard film. I hear her P.R tours are sold out.

Rooney: We are about half way through filming on "Babes in Arms". They booked us a nationwide P. R. tour. I think we end up in New York. Six live shows a day! Just Judy and me. Oh, and They are trying to improve European sales. So they booked Us for a Royal Command Performance in October in London. We just gotta stop any war. Boy, are we gonna put on a show We'll blast these local yokels out their silly minds. "Are we gonna put on a show!". Say, that's my line in the Babes film.

Scene: **Sub Plo**t. Spread over 3 x scenes between the stars dialogue. Or, in one long scene. *While the stars are chatting, behind the scenes, a young German film technician working on the show meets one of the American dancers in the show. They get on very well. The boy is a brainwashed Nazi, but still has a heart. He can be swayed. But he has been forced by anti peace Nazi agents to sabotage the entertainment. He doesn't tell the girl and is pulled like a tug of war whether to go ahead with plan. He finally tells the girl and decides against. He informs the Production team and security, and the Nazi agents are found and caught. The boy, though is arrested. The stars intervene and he is released. A love song about here.*

Astaire: Well, hello Mr. Cole Porter. Heard you were coming.

Porter: Hello fellows. They asked me to write some special lyrics for a big chorus number. I was in Paris. Noel was there. But he couldn't make it here. He's gone to London now. He is rehearsing his new play. I have his lyrics with me for the same number. Oh, and we both persuaded Django and Stephane and the Hot Club Quintet to come here, and do about 15 minutes. I see we have some Senators and M.P.'s here.

Astaire: What about these huge studios. I could really spread out a Dance number in here. This place is bigger than R.K.O. Hey Mickey. When you doing your number with Judy?

Rooney: Oh, we are on a bit later. Oh, hello Senators. Welcome. How are the Peace Talks going. Can we get anywhere with them?

1st
Senator: It's hard to even get them to come to all the meetings. They cancelled several times. They are a hard nosed lot.

2nd	And just as Europe is coming out of the Great Depression.
Senator:	The U.S. is going to raise money, through a public fund, to Support our European Allies, should the balloon go up.
Rooney:	Bullies! That's all it is! I'd just like to punch their lights out. Their leaders are just empty. All hot air and crap!
2nd	More than just hot air this time, Mickey. These are hard liners.
Senator:	They have chips on their shoulders that they won't get rid of.
Rooney:	Don't they know, we've only got one little life? Life is too short for heavy stuff. Your light is on, and poof, it's gone in a flash!
Porter:	You know, Noel and I were talking about this same thing, the other day. I remember, we agreed that we all have trouble dealing with our demons. That is our own private war. The daily fight. That is battle enough. But then we have to put up with all the battles outside in this bloody world! The wars, the murders. Trying to stay positive, peaceful, busy and happy is not so easy!
Astaire:	Right. Take Busby Berkeley, over there, on stage. He is fighting his demons with alcohol. Not the best method.
Rooney:	Yeah. But at least he is fighting. He is struggling to stay right. What else can you do? Give in to the heavy stuff, and you go down man. When I am in front of the cameras, I often have to put on a bright face. After a late night. Some people say, that is the only bit of real acting I do!

1st

Senator: But you have to fight for the right things. If your neighbour parks his car in your drive, you gotta fight him. Same with Trade, borders, and so on. But what the Germans are trying to do are illegal tactics.

Porter: If it was easy, this heaven and hell battle, we would lose the spice of life. If it was a given, that we were always healthy and positive, we'd lose something. No? And Freud would be out of a job! We are made to fight the enemies inside us and outside. And as Noel said, and I'm inclined to agree, the occasional war is good for the soul. Just like a good shouting match. One good thing about sport. All the shouting and screaming at your team or the Ref. Your frustration and aggression get a good work out. Look at it this way. As Groucho might say, a war, quarrels, can save you money on Psychology fees!

Astaire: Look at Cagney. All that violent action stuff he does, probably helps keep him sane and healthy. The tap dancing does the same for me.

Rooney: Just listen to Judy singing. She puts her whole life into it. What bounce. We need more of that stuff. Ah, right. Judy has finished now.

2nd

Senator: You've got plenty of bounce too, Mickey.

Rooney: Yeah. Cause we love our life. Yeah, I know we got a swell number We're lucky. Sure, most people got a crap hand of cards. But they still got a choice, even then. Aint it up to everyone of us, to keep our lamp burning brightly, sort of thing. You know, just be sort of glad you are alive. Just for starters.

Porter: Well, that's life sorted. Which number are you and Judy doing later?

Rooney: "Good Morning". From 'Babes in Arms'. It's still in production. The song is gonna be a hit. Oh Fred, could you take a look at it when we rehearse it. We got a few steps we do. Maybe you could help improve it. Busby is in a mood. And Judy is so fragile right now. What with her chaotic love life.

Astaire: Sure Mickey. Oh, Glenn Miller is on now. Good band. He's new. He is going down big in the dance halls, back home. Go to go. My rehearsal is coming up. So long.

Scene: Out of shot, Fred and Judy bump into each other, as Judy comes off and Fred goes on. Fred does tap dance and Django and the Quintet play. A real hot jazz number. Judy watches

1st
Senator: Did you know that Pathe are making a newsreel, a sort of Documentary about Europe. Backed by League of Nations. They are doing a bit of filming in the streets, nearby, quite soon. Getting the opinions of local Germans on the situation. Come and join in, if you can.

Garland: Can I go too?

Rooney: Judy! Gosh, you are singing swell darling. I know you are tired.

2nd
Senator: Yes, Miss Garland. If you get the time, come along. Maybe put some questions to the German people.

Garland: Well, I don't know about that. We don't know much about what is going on. But I heard some of the gossip just now. I was chatting to Lana and Groucho. We don't hear too much on the MGM lot. But it does sound terrible. Really scary. You know, we were doing this Oz film. And we are in this enchanted land, where everything is sweet and good. And the director, Mr. Fleming, he was so nice too. Well, there was the Wicked Witch, of course, but.........

Rooney: Judy, sweetheart. Wake up! You are also lovely and good. You are the best. But I'm afraid, this world isn't so good.

1st
Senator: Or maybe, don't wake up Judy. We need all the fun and light We can get. We need more good and lovely feelings in this poor world. And they need to be put out there more. Just like both of you do. It's inspiring stuff. And I don't have to tell Show Biz. folk like you two, that it's needed even more in dangerous times like these. As I said at a Senate Budget Committee Meeting, the other day, we badly need your Injections to fight these infections!

Porter: This German Foreign Minister who is coming. What's he like?

2nd
Senator: Quite civilised. Well spoken. Good English. Academic sort. I think you might like him. He should be here soon. Speak to him. He's open minded, compared to the others. Oh, Groucho

Groucho: Open minded, eh. That means we got a smelly, open cess pit coming. Just joking folks. I overheard a bit of your chat. I was just behind, persuading Lana Turner to be in our current Production, "At the Circus".

I want her to do a bare back ride. She provides the bare back, and I go along for the ride! I have a lot riding on it. By the way Fred, how's your current one going?

Astaire: Oh, Broadway Melody. Yeah, it's fine. On time, on budget. And Ellenor Powell is great. The best dancer.

Groucho: Good. What you were saying before, reminded me of when me and my Brothers were starting off, still working out the act. It was in the 1st World War. And all the craziness. And we just, naturally fell into the craziness. We just brought in more crazy, surreal bits of bizness. The world had gone mad. Logic and decency was going out the window. So we naturally followed the trend, and cashed in.

Phil: Right. We are going on the street now, to do this bit of filming Pathe I'm told some of you stars are interested. Come along by all News means. If there's time, you can ask some questions. Nothing man too pointed. Use tact. Stuff like, "What do you think of the current situation?" Do you think the German Government is really helping the ordinary person? The German public will have heard of most of you, even if they don't show our films here. So, it will be a different angle. "The Stars on a fact finding mission!"

Rooney: Hey, buster. I think we can ask the right questions and show tact. We've had to deal with Louis B. Mayer for years! And because they know us, we may get some straight answers. Come on. We'll do your job for you. What rate are you on? Lead on. Come on Judy, Fred. Coming Groucho?

Scene: a Berlin street. Some of the stars and Phil, the cameraman wander out from film studio. Sunny day. Come across a children's Orphanage. They meet Josephine Baker, the cabaret star, who has retired, and runs the orphanage. Stars and Josephine chat, they play with kids.

Rooney   Some of us would like to sponsor a kid and take back Stateside.

Josephine   Yeah. It would be great. But at moment we are having Visa problems; being orphans and all. Some of the kids are from N. Africa, Martinique and other French colonies. Emigration rules are strict.

Judy   Oh, what a shame. Well, keep in touch. Let us know, and we would love to help out and sponsor them.

The children hug the stars; some are crying and shouting
A noisy parade of Nazi soldiers comes marching down the street

SCENE: (A Berlin street. Pathe News Team is filming questions to passers by, with an interpreter. Some stars and politicians are there)

Phil: Pardon me. Do you think your government is doing the best to raise your standard of living? *(Replies are in background)*

Rooney: We've been out here five minutes. It's obvious the public here are towing the Party line. They are not saying what they really think! They are afraid. It's a waste of time.

Oscar   The answers are all pretty much the same. Different

Levant: people all standard replies. "The government is doing a great job". Not for the surrounding countries. It's a brainwashed Dictatorship. It's like the Hollywood Studio System over here. Only, Germany is not quite as bad as that! I can see Harry Cohn at Columbia getting on with the guys over here!

Rooney: Go on, Judy. Have a go.

Garland: (*Takes the microphone*) Excuse me. Do you think your Government is doing a good job with employment?

1st Public: I speak some English. I know you, Mrs. Garland. Hello.

Garland: Actually, I am Miss Garland. I'm not married, though it's not for want of trying! What do you think of your Government?

1st Public: From where we were, a few years before, things are much better. Jobs, houses, factories. Our leaders do good job.

Garland: You think they are doing a good job? Are there things you don't agree with? And can you tell them?

2nd Public: No. We get strong. People strong. Do good things for us.

Garland: But the land. What about the land you want to take?

2nd Public: It is our land.

Garland: But it's not! What about the people who live there?

1st Public: It is ours. It was our land. We will get back ours.

2nd Public: Yes. No one can stop us. Asking, no good. Take, you get! We take!

Garland: But I heard the people there don't want to be taken over by you. And they got no one to help them. That isn't right.

2nd Public: You Americans and British, you take! Americans kill Indians, Take their land. English take over countries. Make slaves!

Garland: Is it true, Oscar?

Oscar: True. What's true. You can make anything sound true, if you want. W. C. Fields, an alcoholic, says he's a light drinker. May West, still says, "Come up and see me sometime", and she must be over sixty!

Garland: It's not right, Mickey, Phil. Is it? Oh, I don't know.

2nd Public: You take. We do same as you. Go. Your film, no want here.

Garland: My god, you are so stupid! You ignorant bunch of idiots! You pig headed baboons! I can't talk to you. You won't listen. There are two sides you know! I'm not wasting my time with you. Phil, it's stupid, horrible!

Phil: Come on Judy. Leave it. Mickey……

Garland: ……..Oh, no. I'm getting giddy…..

Rooney: I don't want you upset. Are you gonna faint?

Garland: I'm tired. Take me back. (Judy, Mickey walk back to Studios)

SCENE: Film Studios (In Judy's dressing room. There's a bed)

Garland: Okay, Mickey. See you in a bit. We'll do our number. A short nap will help. I'll get over it. Those idiots! Come and get me.

Mickey: Okay darling.

*(Judy Garland lies down and falls asleep. And dreams. **This is her Dream**. Judy is flying around in the sky, or on a fabled flying creature, 'Answerous'. (Or on a magic carpet, or by Herself) As she passes clouds, they change shape and become famous figures in History. Great men. Judy calls out questions, as she passes them. They reply briefly, in their own ways. The famous figures are: Plato, Oscar Wilde, Descartes, Woody Allen, Wagner, Goethe, Beethoven, Da Vinci and John Lennon)*

Garland: Oh my. Lions and Witches and creepy things. Lions and Witches and scary things. Oh my. Oh, hi there. How do I stop being scared, Mr. Plato?

Plato: Put on some red socks, and fill them full of holes. And if you have some red shoes, that would be a great help.

Garland: That's no help. That's silly. And he's a clever man? Oh hi There, Mr. Oscar Wilde. When I'm scared, and I want to hide and give up, how do I say, "No", and plough on?

Wilde: No. A farmer ploughs on. In a field. You must just plough on. Somehow. No choice. Often what you think you are scared of isn't so bad. It's just your own scariness inside you. Remember when the Wicked

Witch wants to get you, and bring you down, it's just a figment of your fevered imagination It's not real, just thoughts. So, Judy, don't give a fig for it. Humbug it. Your diamond, encrusted heart in your beating Soul, is worth two in the bush. Especially, the late, departed President Bush. And remember, if you are in your boudoir, taking off your dress, ready for bed, and a man comes in and 'tries it on' with you, you can be sure he's a Transvestite!

Garland: Oh! Well, thanks, Mr. Wilde. But what if all around me are Bullies and Black Witches, pressing to bring me down? Oh, Mr. Descartes, what should I do then?

Descartes: Well, there are two opposite sides to everything in the Universe. Exceptions are wealthy Football Clubs. In which case there is a third side. Money. Beside that, and besides, a glass of Cider will quench the two sides of an equalateral. It is a simple case of Metamorphic Existentialism, not Residual Pantheism. Or, do what I do. Ignore them, or kick 'em in the teeth! On this, I refer you to Mr. Woody Allen, at the next cloud.

Allen: You see, Judy, although I use philosophy a lot in my films, this is not the time or place. And I'm not in time or place either. This is 1939, when I was only 2 years old. But I am here from the future, because the author needed some jokes here. This play was getting too serious and wearing thin. Like Yul Brynner's hair. So, I noticed you were getting upset, a couple of pages back. You got scared and angry, and this is why you are dreaming. I can think of more exciting things to dream about! But yeah. All this bad stuff. What to do? Well you got to have some rough or life would be too dull, too routine. Like making love to a perfect woman, day after day, after day after......Well, there are better examples I could have used!

Garland: Hey, buster. What kind of answer is that supposed to be? Where did they drag you out from? Cloud cuckoo land? And in thirty years time, they will say your are a genius! I am dreaming because I am confused, and dreams are supposed to give you answers. Snap out of it genius, and give!

Allen: Precocious, nosey little kid, aren't you. Feeling giddy flying round and round. Good! But keep looking East, kid. That's where hope lies. And you are one of the great inspirational leaders of giving hope. And you always will be.

Garland: Well, I guess so Woody. I am that kind of person. You know, Just so very glad to be alive. But you have so much to say, you are the precocious one here. I have to ask questions. It's that kind of dream. And you aren't that funny. I've been on Bob Hope's radio show, and he's funnier.

Allen: He has a team of gag writers. Hope just acts!

Garland: Darn it! Still no clear answers. Mr. Wagner, I hear you are something to do with all the terrible things going on round here. All the bullying. Don't like it. My mother bullied me and sometimes locked me in rooms. Bad things like that. And I am getting to be a temperamental star, and learning how to get my own way. I can wrap the film staff round my finger. How do we stay happy and positive? Quick answer please.

Wagner: Compose operas six hour long. Makes me happy. They bore the pants off the audience. They pretend to know, but they are Poseurs. Long operas make my accountant happy too.

Garland: I like what I do too.

Wagner: I know. Keep on. You are lucky.

Garland: And keep flying?

Wagner: My "Flying Dutchman" didn't stop to worry. He just kept on.

Garland: Think less?

Wagner: Yes. All these questions, doubts. Don't need 'em. And I didn't create the Third Reich. Just wrote that Jews were the trouble makers, and that Germans were the Master race!

Garland: Gosh! It's only human to have questions, isn't it, Mr. Goethe?

Goethe: You're asking again. That's the problem.

Garland: What?

Goethe: The whole human bit. We are so much more than questions.

Garland: You mean, Angels?

Goethe: Well, you are, already. But most people have to dig and dig to find their gold. And keep finding.

Garland: And when they find it, what do they do?

Goethe: Give out, enjoy it, give it out. Like Spring sunshine, like happy, running Rivers. Go with that flow. Go, go, go!

Garland: Go with the flow, Mr. Goethe?

Goethe: Cherish it. It will feed on itself and grow more, brighter. Like compound interest.

Garland: I'm not allowed a bank account.

Goethe: It's just cracking the habit. Getting unstuck, and stronger than the opposite forces.

Garland: The dark, painful stuff?

Goethe: Yes. You know, one day they will use that. "May the Force be with you". That's what it means.

Garland: The Force and magic life. Ain't it great!

Goethe: Yes. But one day they will change that too. Lawyers will rub their hands and say, "May di - vorce be with you!"

Garland: Thanks, Mr. Goethe. You're a breeze. Byeeee. Hi Mr. Beethoven. Got a word on this?

Beethoven: I got genius. You got genius. Everybody got.....Well, it helps to keep you going. Brandy does too. Don't let all this get you down. And this is all happening in my own Country too! This is 1939. But I guarantee, in the year 2000, it will be the same. Nothing will change. The same terrible things will happen.

Garland: You are a breeze too, Mr Beethoven. Oh, hi Mr. Da Vinci.

Da Vinci: Now hold on Judy. Don't get carried away. There are problems. So keep your feet on the ground.

Garland: Like the Great Depression, or the Crash of 1929.

Da Vinci:　Er, yes. And like our Leaders to come. They will still be a real problem. Fundamentally unable to do the job. Meaning they will have the funds, but be mentally unable.

Garland:　God, how many more of these cloud people are there? Oh my. You are quite young, er, Mr. John Lennon.

Lennon:　What we need here is a big T.L.C. Machine. Where ever there is someone brewing up trouble, stick them in the machine and it gives them lots and lots of big hugs and cuddles, till the trouble melts away. That's all bullies need. Love and care.

Garland:　You think it would work?

Lennon:　If 'Trouble People' feel loved and needed, then it will be peaceful, and we can all get on with the serious business of having some fun around here!

Garland:　Gosh, what's that noise?

(Suddenly, from out of dark clouds, comes a black, Amorphous shaped monster. It flies towards Judy, on her fabled creature, 'Answerous'. It comes nearer.

And the noise It is making is just one loud, scary sound, over and over, "Paralyse yer, paralyse yer, paralyse yer!" Judy is terrified and starts to fly away. The Paralyser comes after, as in all monster nightmares)

Garland:　Help me, help, help someone! No, oh no, no!

(As they fly around the sky, The Paralyser catches Judy. Part of its mass knocks into Judy, trying to engulf her and drop her out of the sky, to plunge her to her death. It keeps banging into her. Bang, bang, bang! Judy slowly wakes up. Bang, bang.............

Rooney: *(Banging on Judy's dressing room door)* Judy, are you there? Open up. It's me, Mickey.

Garland: Oh Mickey, give me a hug. God, that was scary. I don't ever want that again. Gosh, I'm glad to be back with you all again! I had the this terrible dream, Mickey........

Rooney: Tell me later, honey. We going to meet the German Foreign Minister. He's just come.

Oscar There you are. What happened to you? Everyone is saying what an important part of the Mission this is, to talk to this Foreign Minister. He's an open minded guy, so we can talk to him sort of straight, but use tact. We mustn't upset him.

(They walk back to the main hall area. Announcements)

Announcer: Welcome to the German Foreign Minister, Herr Rip van off. He is off duty, and has come to watch and enjoy rehearsals. Thanks to The Quintet of the Hot Club for their 15 minutes. Thanks Django and Stephane. Your slot will go down really well. It's different. Next, the Marx Brothers. Chico and Groucho are still working on their act, with the script writers. So let's hear what you've got so far boys. They won't be using all of this material. It's a mini sample, right Groucho?

Groucho: That's our Mother's name, Minnie. Are you slurring off my Mother's honour? A duel, Sir. You agree? Then it's Adieu Sir. This part is mostly me. Chico may come in later. Played golf the other day. My mother in law was with us, and She moaned the whole way round. She dropped the clubs twice! Here's an example of mixed feelings: My mother in Law drove my brand new car over a cliff! * I opened the door. My mother in law was standing on the front step. She said, "Can I stay here tonight?" I said, "Yes", and slammed the door.*

* My mother in law moaned in the car, all the way from the Supermarket. So I let her out of the boot. Ah, the missing link

Chico: Hey, boss. I heard they gotta a new fuel for cars. They gonna burn rubbish. And I heard they gonna use your act!

Groucho: You know, if they ever make ignorance a capital offence, I don't give much for your chances. Tell me, what was that small business you started. How is it doing?

Chico: I'm a keeping chickens, and a making umbrellas.

Groucho: I know it's a silly question, but what for?

Chico: I'm a making a little nest egg for a rainy day!(17)

Groucho: It's when there is a crisis, like the Great Depression of the 30's, that you need humour. Or when there is a shipwreck. A comedian would have gone down well on the Titanic?

Chico: We were at the top of our game in the Depression.

Groucho: I rest my case.

Chico: Why do you put it here?

Groucho: What?

Chico: Your case. Put it over there. It's in the way.

Groucho: This proves my point. Insanity is back in fashion. And I give him the benefit of the doubt, that he is a man.... of a fashion.

Chico: Hygiene is important. Why is In - Sanitation so popular?

Groucho: Let me just go on a bit more. Back in the States, the musical Composer, Frank Lesser and his wife, are not very nice People. It is said that his wife is the Evil of two Lessers. The Foreign Minister may not have got that one, although I know his English is excellent.

              A friend told me that, last year, he gave his wife a special Birthday present. A silver and fur lined coffin. This year his Wife asked him, "You didn't get me a birthday present" And he said, "No. You haven't used last year's present yet". Well, that's some of the act. We are still knocking it into shape.

Announcer: Thanks Groucho. We are going to have a break in Rehearsals, now. The Foreign minister, Herr Rip van Off has asked us to see some newsreel footage about modern Germany. He assures us, it is not propaganda, but is to show The Goodwill Mission how well Germany is doing. Be seated Everyone. Screen. Lights. Roll it.

(Newsreels of life in Germany is shown. But it includes film Of Huge Fascist Rallies and Military Parades. Contrary to the Foreign Minister's assurances. There are some, quiet murmurs in the watching audience. The politicians watch, uncomfortably, but show tact. One voice from the audience cannot control her feelings. An emotional Judy)

Garland: What the hell is going on. This looks like propaganda to me. You told us there wouldn't be any, Minister. We are here, to Help get some goodwill going with your country. Some trust. Stop anything unfriendly between us. And what do you do. Pour this down our throats. How powerful you are. Well two Can play at that game! It's got to stop. It's like a volcano.

Rooney: Judy, sit down, for God's sake. Sorry folk. Judy is tired and she just had a bad dream. Come on Judy...........

Garland: No, I won't. Someone's got to tell them. Will God agree with all this? Is He looking? Does He know? Why do you waste your precious lives on war and hate? It has got to stop. I can't sing for these men! I will choke! If the world is like this, I can't sing, I won't sing! I've sung Lovely songs. Fred has, Mickey too. And Cole writes the Most wonderful songs. Why won't all the music wash away the hate? All this horrible, mad stuff, up there on the Screen. Why can't you Ministers lighten up? Get out and Swing like Fred Astaire. Dance your blues away. Get your Other leaders here. I'll knock some sense into them! Life is too short! Let's do that. Let's do, "All God's Children Got Rhythm" like Harpo did in, "Day At The Races".

We'll all dance around Berlin, us Yanks, the Brits and the German people. We'll dance it away. Laugh it away. Life is too short. Oh, god. You are all looking at me as if I am crazy.

2nd Senator:	Your heart is in the right place, Judy. But it has to be done through talking, negotiation. So we can come to a common understanding. And mutual trust.

Oscar: She is seeing it through show business eyes. Politicians work in a more methodical way, Judy. Some say, in mysterious ways. But we must let them thrash it out. Only way we have.

Garland: *(She carries on regardless, inspired, heart felt and emotional)*

No. It doesn't work. The Politicians are acting, pretending They say they all want to get on. But the talking just goes on And on. If they were happy people and really loved life, they Would sit and talk and clear up any problems just like that. And they would spend the rest of the time, joking, singing, Dancing and hugging! That's how it should be. But they are Not happy. So they go the other way, like up on the screen Now. They want power. The tanks, the soldiers.....It's too horrible. I can't live in a world like this.

(The newsreel film is still playing on the screen. The Army Parades, planes, tanks, the hysteria at Rallies. Judy Garland jumps up, runs up on to the stage, grabs the microphone, and, over the noise of the German Army machine, and protests from the German Delegation, she sings the song....

Garland: "Somewhere over the rainbow..............

(Curtain!)

27.10.17

TRAUMA

Safe, she loves me, but suddenly, turns into a Bogeyman and Banshee. Help scream horror; someone save me take me out this conflict hell..
I run I hide, terrified, a nightmare, no courage
This the trauma catalyst I'm shaking. row after row of headless ogres. Horrified she'll get me she insists

Coward to face punishment other side of door.
What did I do; what's it for?
Emotional numbness self esteem crushed like car crusher
Trembling, yet like stone rooted to spot
undecided I can't face alone what's on other side of door
What did I do, what's if for
Makes torture worse innocent but hell is out to get me
HELP Someone save me come take me out this frozen undecided state
If i had the courage to face punishment
Would have no disgrace shame trauma feel a man head up
Not have PTSD [Post Traumatic Stress Disorder]
Feel coward down to marrow harrowing

I avoid rows bullies bossy people. Cant deal with them. Hide in parks alleys doorways country walks; cross road to avoid
Carry fear of bossy people everywhere go
Fear of trauma repeat just below surface; ready to flinch cower volcano of red hot fears
Post trauma; realized potential envious bullies want to punish,

hurt emotionally. Equivalent of using weapons to hurt.
Non stop sea ocean of sharks have to learn protect self or fight back
The sensitive, poetic heart being is under constant attack
Found friend in creativity a healer real life state beyond reach of bullies and hate

I could describe trauma in detail but decided do me no good
Like poking finger in wound and saying look see the blood
Talking about effect of post trauma better.

You won't agree but I know I've more courage, had to have, than hero of VC medal winner many times over. I know
I'm in league same boat, but much worse and longer with Holocaust, Genocide, war accident bullied victims. Yes I can say that. And know it. **Daily** suffering pain torture fear, misery for 70 years
You laugh you will disagree; be angry. But just try it for long lifetime every day try it and see.
I've had to have more tenacity guts to hang keep going long lifetime every day
With my fears. Not just few days or years what medal do I get
Just to keep going facing with fears active running into battle facing enemy guns rattle
Just going out door daily is like that over and over facing fears with PTSD
Stayed in doors painting listening to Bach safe peaceful away from noisy battle
I'm in a war zone, hurt and bleeding terrified alone

Unfreezing emotional numbness all little wires of feeling connections
Have to be defrosted to work
To all you reading this, who sometimes feel afraid lost unsure disconnected you'll get some idea what I mean say and every day non stop
I know you may say we all go thru that PTSD is much more

Work at writing any creative art but particular write despite the numbness
Write words is hot water to defrost frozen feelings, connections.

To get you feeling and a whole person
Joined supportive communities; empathetic friends

Once the wound was begun, the smell and sight of blood was a
magnet to the pure venomous and envious bullies trod over my
crushed spirit and broken body and laughed all of life
With no open wound would not be victim
That's my life struggle Not overcome yet but still hanging in trucking on
Healers counsellors many hundreds of others helped a bit to keep
going
Desperate Phone calls to a friend on freezing wet nights
Volunteers staff understanding supportive helps Painting writing
helps step by step to strengthen self esteem self belief

Coward to marrow harrowing. row after row of headless men ogres
out to get me
Can't avoid it. For first few years It was creamy peachy at home.....
then......
Suddenly she turns into a Bogeyman and Banshee
I run, hide, terrified, a nightmare
This the trauma catalyst. Horrified she'll get me she insists! I'm
shaking.
Emotional numbness; self esteem squeezed flat like a car crusher
I was innocent, but if I had the courage to face punishment,
the trauma would not have happened.
Makes torture worse; innocent but hell is out to get me
I could hide and protect my trauma, my creative secret

Found friend in creativity a healer real life state beyond reach of
bullies and hate
So everywhere every day had to face prospect of being traumatized
by people
Avoid rows bullies bossy people cant face them hide in parks alleys
doorways country walk and walk alone cross road.
Carry fear of people everywhere go
Fear of trauma repeat just below surface ready to flinch cower
volcano of red hot fears
You won't agree but I know I've more courage than hero of VC
medal winner 100 times over I know
I'm in league same boat with Holocaust, Genocide, war accident
bullied victims

You laugh you may disagree be angry Try it for long lifetime every day try it and see

I've had to have more tenacity guts to hang keep going long lifetime every day

With my fears. Not just few days or years what medal do I get

Just to keep going facing with fears active running into battle facing enemy guns rattle

Just going out door daily is like that over and over facing fears with PTSD

Stayed in doors painting listening to Bach safe peaceful away from noisy battle

I'm in a war zone, hurt and bleeding terrified alone

Unfreezing emotional numbness all little wires of feeling connections

Have to be defrosted to work

To all you reading this, who sometimes feel afraid lost unsure disconnected you'll get some idea what I mean say and every day non stop

I know you may say we all go thru that PTSD is much more intense!

Once the wound was begun, the smell and sight of blood was a magnet to the pure venomous and envious bullies trod over my crushed spirit and broken body and laughed all of life

With no open wound would not be victim

That's my life struggle Not overcome yet but still hanging in trucking on

Healers counsellors many hundreds of others helped a bit to keep going Desperate Phone calls to a friend on freezing wet nights

Volunteers staff understanding supportive helps Painting writing helps step by step to strengthen self esteem self belief

NO CONTROL [WHO'S IN CHARGE HERE?]

I know you're busy, but this won't take long.
I must share this, to help me right a wrong.
They say, "you are in charge; make your own bed?"
(Sing the next four lines to the Irving Berlin tune)
"They say that being in charge is wonderful,
It's wonderful, so they tell me.
I can't recall who said it.
I know I never read it " .... do you know the song?

Well, from my experience,
That's nonsense!
Who takes control of their lives? How many?
Okay. Sinatra did it his way. But who else?
How many build their destiny?
Who is master of their fate,
Captain of a ship.
Me? No. I still can't even see my hand of cards.
Tony Blair? Well no. I don't include retards!

Remember your childhood.
That's when you learn to drive your car?
Not me. If yours was anything like mine,
You were being fattened up for a Temple type sacrifice.
A sacrifice too far.
Fattened for a family meal.
A meal to make a force fed piggy squeal.
A meal to feed the family kudos.
A brainwashed meal, as cute as; Reflected glory in my triumph.

96

So the family can shout, "Our son, oh yes, he's no chump!"
And cheer, with arms raised and chest out pride,
"You've made us proud son".
God, who is taking who for a ride.

My test? To win the; "I AM A SON OF THE COMMANDMENT"
approved seal.
The; "NOW I AM A MAN" test, "with proper gent appeal!"
Over the years, the Temple brass blew louder.....oompha, oompha.
As the tests grew nearer;
My school exams and bar mitzvah.

Drive my car? Ha! Am I in control? Ha ha!
Not even control of my sweating and shaking limbs.
Did I want a Barmitzvah? No! Was I asked?
It has no meaning or sense to me.
My Leviticus sedra, was all about Kashrut laws.
I'm still no expert on them.
No 'SHELL' fish?
What's that? No fish in oil?

And I studied for 2 years!
My Barmitzvah took 2 hours to sing my way through,
And I wasn't doing things 'My Way'.
My bar mitzvah teacher was a Jewish fundamentalist.
('Mental' being the operative word)
Would have made a great terrorist fanatic for the other side,
If he hadn't been Jewish.

He threatened me. "You must do a wonderful Barmitzvah.
Make me proud, make your parents proud, your whole family, the
whole community",
(He may have asked me to make the whole of Israel proud, I don't
remember)
"Give your family pride. "If you don't", he threatened, "I'll shoot you,
and bury you in the rubbish heap at the end of the garden, with the
rats!"
I have no idea if this was for compost.

With this encouragement, I made them proud.
I was sewn and trussed up like a fattened pig.

To top off my humiliation, I had to do a thank you speech! God!
Had to thank lots of people. Even ones I didn't like.
Like my grandmother. She once told my mother, "Your son will
never get anywhere.
It might have helped if she had told me where to go!
Come to think of it, she did.
That speech too, was for family kudos; reflected glory.
It's like a nation gets a boost when their football team does well.
Okay, England is an exception!

So where did the; "I am in control" bit fit?
I had to do it. Where's the "I did it my way" bit?
I didn't like the dry mouth, the panic, the fear of failure.
Letting my parents down. Though if I could have strung them up,
I probably would have let them down!
All the polite, "please and thank you's". All the, "Yes mine Fuhrer"

All the pinched cheeks and, "Have you been a good boy?" that I
had to endure.
What was I, a number 11 going in to save the game?
Or the Dutch boy, who saved Holland with his finger in the dyke
fame.
What was this: a competition between families?
"My parents would say, "My boy did a wonderful Bar mitzvah. Did it
beautiful. Made us so proud!"

"My boy did a wonderful Barmitzvah. He made us so proud.
Our boy he passed with top grades. He has a place at Grammar
School
Oh, did our boy do a wonderful Sedra. He did it beautifully.
Listen, even a good roast chicken don't get praise like this.
But like chickens, I was stuffed, hook line and stinker.

But my exam failure, not going to Grammar School, they would not
say that out loud.
A good roast chicken don't get pride and praise like my parents
puffed up breasts.
But like chickens, I was stuffed, hook line and stinker.
[Or is that turkeys?]

Where did the sweat and trembling get me?
And the, "Now I am a man!"
Am I head of a company? Have I got a house, car, wife, friends?
What did it do? This mindless, brainwashed tradition. What was it for?
If I had refused to do the 11+ exam or bar mitzvah?
If I'd said to my parents," No. Don't like my legs shaking,
My tummy falling out. Don't like the knife edge fretting".
If I'd been like Oliver Twist, gone against the rules, done the unexpected,
Then I might well be head of a company by now.
Might not have lost confidence, been a nervous wreck.
What a terrible toll. A Sacrifice for what the heck?

I was devastated when I failed. I should have passed easily. Brains in spades.
I wanted a good education. Clever at school; good grades.
Listen guys. You wanted to give me a test to prove I was a man?
I could have jumped off tall trees, like jungle tribes can.
Why didn't you leave me naked on some freezing hill top, Spartan like?
That makes sense!
If I survived, that would have proved something, wouldn't it?
But the pressure cooker of making the family proud.
Not letting the family down. The family name! That makes me wild!
That's a recipe for disaster, a breakdown for a fractured child.

There were, it's true, some bonuses. These came from buying into the mindless sacrifice:
1st Bonus: I acquired several phobias. My fears kept me off the streets. I was afraid to go out. So, at least I was safe.
I became a professional nervous wreck at age 11
Okay I was already on the way. I'd had a good training from start
By 11, I was already hyper sensitive and frightened
No mind of my own. Good, obedient from fear. Great Bonus!

2nd Bonus: I had a pretty good record: 1 pass, 1 failure.
Oh and another pass, I forgot: I survived the war.
But even in that pass, I had no control.
I had no control or say in what Hitler had for breakfast,

Over his moustache, clothes, or world policies.

3ʳᵈ Bonus: They told me, "Today you are a man".
Good. So I tried to get into nightclubs,
but my short trousers gave me away!
Took my Barmitzvah cheques to buy a car. No go. Went to Soho to
a Pro. Even there, no 'quid pro quo'!
She said she'd see me when my voice broke.
I told her, I was already a broken man.

But with these free bonuses for being a man, I noticed I still had to
eat my greens, the fat on the meat; I still had to come in for dinner
on time.
How the hell was that being in charge?
And, it wasn't even me who decided, "Now I am a man." It was
them!
And besides, I knew I wasn't. I wasn't even man enough to believe
I was a man.
Officially I was. I had performed the ceremony. Passed the tests.
But I knew I was the man who wasn't.
Like the film, "The Man Who Never Was".
Though, from the title, he had been a man once. I never even got
that far.

Yet, I had been declared a man. It was in the papers; the notices.
Then they were all wrong? But I could see I was an invisible man.
No wonder I couldn't rebel or take charge?
There was no me! Ah! I see! No wonder driving a car was hard.
It's hard enough when you have a you. But I've been an invisible
person trying to drive an invisible car!
I'd done the rituals. Now I was a responsible man, but I knew it was
hollow.
Guilt, deception, pretence took their turns to drive me.
I hid the truth. Yes, I could easily have gone into politics.
Mmmmmm. "Now you are a man." Oh, really? Mmmmmmmm.

Like all our childhoods, mine wasn't all bad. The first 9 months were
okay! I do have some good memories, like; Weekend family visits,
my plump, avaricious aunts; cigar smoke filled rooms, the endless
card games, the tea trolley, the sunlit peace of a Victoriana room,
the gardens, the smell of post war car seat leather, my father's
boxed hats wrapped in rustling, white tissue paper, the smell of the
steam presses, and playing with hatpins and a magnet,

Oh yes, and the sun shining over the school playing fields, and feeling clean and bright, the radio shows, belonging to a family and the few friends I had………..
Same as yours, not all bad.

But I was treated like a battery hen, a gladiator, force fed and trussed, without a say.
The family and tradition knew where I was going, and what for. But not me.
Not being in charge of my life, I was not enjoying the emasculation.
Rather the terror of Hitler's bombs raining down,
Than the terror of failing exams.
Rather the dread of those Doodlebug bombs coming over
Than the dread of learning fractions and grammar.
Or the panic of learning those funny musical signs above the Hebrew words.
The Israelites, slaves in Egypt, had an easier time!
But after I finish writing this out of my system, it will break the spell.
Give me a brainwash detox. Out, out dam packing me in your Traditional box.
All based on a bunch of fairy tales by ancient 'holy' bards. Ancient Bards? Ha, no! Manipulative retards!

"Yes, I want to break free, I must break free, free of the power over me, Break free, and be the real me", like Queen sang.
I'll hatch out of that egg, use my wings. Steer the ship my way …..
drive my own car. If I can get a car of my own.

Would have preferred to play football on Saturday with friends,
But I, from fear of my religious teacher went dutifully to Temple.
And the friends, who only did five minute bar mitzvahs, Who disobeyed their parents and teachers too, are now heads of companies!
But I was a good boy, a dutiful toy, making my bed to others plans,
It's hands down, you won't stand a chance.
"Hey, take a glance at that golden statue of a perfect boy,
As good as gold, over there on that plinth. … . It's a synch he was no trouble.
A cert he got no dirt on his hands. But no mind or feelings of his own.
Never a real person, with passions and emotions.

Too afraid, too concerned about giving his parents a trouble free
life".

The way I was bought up, was safe, easy, it would seem.
No hardships, no hunger, and some peaches and cream. Suddenly,
I'm told to go in and bat for the family.
And don't dare let them down. But my safe life caught me with my
pants down.
Off guard. No toughness, no fight. I was bright, but it was too much
to bear.
Too much burden. No want. Not fair?

Like most people, probably you too, we have to be cleared out.
Detoxed from things which are not us. The influenza process.
Nature does it too.
Painful stuff that makes us sick. Being forced to endure
experiences foreign,
And take a long journey into the night, to clear out, to become our
own bright day.

Yes, I know. You were too young. But it's a metaphor. What for?
What are your metaphors for if you can't mix your metaphors.
I get my kicks when there's a mix.
Well, I am seemingly, brimming, dare I say, I daresay, with ideas;
Being snappy and apt, with happy phrases, which a sincere writer
embraces
Time to get wise and prioritise. Let's see. What's priority?
Not poetry. Find a wife? No, it's life.
No more the blank, subservient boy page
Time to get up on life's dangerous, adventurous stage
No more the obedient page
More the king must be my next thing
Not the art of poetry, but the art of living

Who decides what's good and bad? Only us. If it's true real from
our being hearts
Then that's bottom line. Can be criticised; told it's rubbish, but we
know it came from a real place And we have to live with ourselves,
our conscience; and we have to massage an audience with laughs
or pleasing stuff. A bit yeah, but please and be true to your feelings,
integrity **first.**

Who decides what's good bad? Only us. If it's true real from our being hearts
Then that's bottom line. Can be criticised told it's rubbish, but we know it came from a real place And we have to live with ourselves our conscience And why do we have to rub massage an audience with laughs or pleasing stuff ahhhhhhh stuff? A bit yeah, but please self first. Stuff that comes out / produce is best when comes from our being, sincere, straight like animals and children.

1. 12. 17

PURE LOVE INSIDE

You want it, you got it; not out there, in here; time to repeat. you know the pure love we seek is the closest thing we got.
we carry it as a baby.
Focus on the love in you and if you're in love, that too!

We find love; is that pure love?
Sooner or later, somehow, something gets in the way.
It takes the smallest thing to lacerate the eloquence of that love.
Momentary joy is crushed under black titanic clouds.
That love we had vapourizes into air; we are felled love is rejected, our pleasure repelled
We gush onwards again to smash the rampart walls to find and extract any small tincture of love
The attack fails; we repeat. Result: madness, anger, heartbreak!!

Why all the love poems and songs; "don't go, come back".
Each word you write has the elemental drive to feel and share love.
We have to find ways to express powerful love we feel.
We cling, "don't go", desperate; not healthy.

The desperate thirst to feel love drives men to desperate acts

The natural force to feel love creates our collisions, explosions of deadly gases the gigantic rolling and thrusting of winds, tornadoes.

That's why, if love goes bad, there's such a dangerous mad frustrating fall out; we're so thirsty drives crazy in a cruel empty desert.

Don't care if this a proper poem; time to scream out loud, while suffering, crime goes on, right now; refugees, children!! largely because focus to get love is out there, not in here.
Yes time to be angry and shout, "you're going the wrong way!!"

You want it, you got it; not out there, in here; time to repeat the way it is.
You know, the pure love we seek is the closest thing we got.
we carry it as a baby. Focus on the love in you and if you're in love, that too.
Try all ways to enjoy and feel great.
Be less disappointed flower carries within its scent that we enjoy
But and so we rush to scale the ramparts with with furious intensity
Or gently like a soothing summer breeze.

We meet love is that pure love
then sooner or later somehow something gets in the way
It takes the smallest thing to lacerate the eloquence of that love
Our hearts are lacerated
our momentary joy is crushed under black titanic clouds we are left empty as graves
That love we had vapourizes into air; we are felled; the defenders reject; the attack is repelled.
We gush onwards again to smash the rampart's walls to find and extract any small tincture of love
The attack fails. Result; madness anger heartbreak
Always exceptions.

We pick selves up and attack once more to find love
We find, it fails; we search again; we find, it fails.
Can I talk I have no one can't find love no one.
How can I talk the subject is pure love not clinging liking someone
Why all the love poems and songs, "don't go", "come back."
Each word you write has the elemental drive to feel and share love
We have to find a vehicle to express powerful love we feel for the love to go
We cling, "Don't go!", desperate not healthy,
In that desperation to feel love is the thirst that drives men to acts of ugly desperation.

We see in the news,
Yes, time to be angry and shout, "You're going the wrong way!"
The natural force, urge to feel love creates in us, can you feel
the collisions, explosions, eruptions of planets the spewing out of
deadly gases, the gigantic rolling and thrusting
Of winds, tornadoes. That's why if love goes bad, there's such a
dangerous, mad, frustrated fall out. Being so thirsty, drives you
crazy; in a cruel, empty desert, we lose!
Membranes punctured.

Time to scream out loud, while suffering, death goes on, right now;
refugees, children…….. All because the focus to feel love is out
there, not in here!

12.3.11

COULD HAVE BEEN

Is the grass always greener? Have others got what we have not?
Have we been dealt a rubbish hand?
Please change this attitudinal stricture.
Lift your heads and see the wider picture.

Take notes please;
Hunger, disease, unemployment.
Charity which goes to the Army and the Government.
Imprisonment, torture and cruelty;
Suffering from natural disasters;
Wars and riots are just angry human plasters!

On one hand there's volcanic eruption.
On the other, my brother, is human corruption.
Cruelties that will be repeated on those who come after us.
Not solved; but repeated and repeated.

Problems with Ecology, and Economy.
[From the Latin: 'You have a con a me!']
Repeated problems which won't go.
Unnecessary pain due to the greedy ego!
The terrible twins; Eco. and Eco.
A poor echo of us Eco Homos.

But you know there's enough food and money
To solve all hunger and poverty.
If just ten per cent

From all the millionaires, is sent,
Along with farming experts,
To teach and train,
The deserts can bloom.
With all pulling together, And an unselfish will, it can't fail.
Look, what they've done in the land of Israel!

If there were Comparison sites to compare our lot,
We might pray and say, "Thank my lucky stars for what I got!"
Look around, watch the news.
It might help to change your jealous views.

For a start, we're on dry land, not wrecked by sea.
If told to live in someone else's shoes,
To live their lives, would we refuse?
Yes, the grass is not necessarily greener.
But, wait. I've been an early morning toilet cleaner,
I've seen the seedier side.
So sometimes the grass IS greener. Sorry I lied!

Yes, I've been a busy, underpaid little elf, and on the shelf.
[I leave that off my C.V. Keep it to myself!]
Could have been a steel worker, heavy and hot.
Or a soldier in the Army, who gets himself shot.
Or in a poor family, slaving all day in a rice field
Or a sex worker, arrested, but who's Pimp has appealed.

A sardine commuter, in front of a computer
A wrongly imprisoned prisoner of conscience.
Amnesty tries, but says there's no chance.
Could be in a band at Ibezian raves.
Or one of the hoards of white collar slaves, With everything going
from worse to badder.
He's no chance to get on the mortgage ladder.

Could have been a bankrupt farmer from a poor crop yield.
Or a laid off policeman, who loses gun and shield
Could be a show biz entertainer, on a retainer
Who's dropped from the cast.
You're only as good as your last!

Or a baggage handler, who must work in rain and frost
No wonder our bags get lost.

Had some sense and avoided the marriage nonsense.
Two and half kids; I've seen the poor sods. Life not your own. So far
escaped, thank the gods.
Could be a cement mixer; a sports betting fixer
I've worked on farms; slept well, but with aching legs and arms.
I've dug up gardens and dug up roads
Done office work in several different modes

Could have been in a family of Royals,
Fleecing the nation, keeping the spoils.
Or could be an accountant on call
For clients political.
Creating bookkeeping blunders.
They help themselves, when they should help us!

One wonders.... no, it's too farcical....
But I read about this in a newspaper article,
The Board Chairman of a company,
Which he runs as if he owns as his,
Has refused to take his annual bonuses!
Is he riddled by conscience?
Or is it just a bit of Lewis Carroll, publicity nonsense.

Just remember these examples when we wish we could have
been a......
Or whenever we think the grass is greener........

Both Prince Andrew and Fergie are social hangers on.
Greasy, social climbers who tend to get it wrong.
President Obama turns national problems into his own private
drama
Osama bin Larden seems far calmer, so we glean.
But that's because he's absent, and never seen.

Katy Price tries to keep looking lovely and nice, with plastic surgery
at any price.
Liz Taylor ran through several husbands and face lifts,

Paid from her limited acting gifts.
Belasconi runs the country like a brothel and like The Mafia
Kerri Katona hasn't one talented bone inside her.
I know this is a mish mash of ideas
A Harem of eclectic idiosyncrasies
Ideas about our dreams and fears
About how we cross these dangerous seas.
Fact of the matter, I needed a natter;
A moan to you on the phone
Although after this chat, I must say, I feel even flatter.

But remember, when you make that, "I'm fed up" call, it's a miracle
there's life on Earth at all.
But if you do have a bad hand in life, I won't scoff.
Just remember, you could still be worse off.
You may wish you had been a Gazelle, not a Hyena.
But try to accept the you that you are.
Or would you rather be poor, or at war in Syria!

24.9.2017

NATURE AND NEWS
[1ST DRAFT]

Through the window, a fiery rust red tree dazzles.
It shares the garden with demure yellow foliage.
And larger trees of multi greens under a milky grey sky.
And on my desk a newspaper filled with the usual madness.
How can sensitive people survive with this ugly noise!
Wake up, I'll have my say; do we, here, feel the same way?
Those gorgeous trees, understated, true, for all to enjoy;
While hiding in its leaves, the paper spews lies and sinister dramas.

At the foot of the trees I see white naked babies crawling around a
naked mother; A metaphor for the elemental energy of life.
The reds and greens are beautiful musical harmonies
The news doesn't sing; just splutters discordant mania.
How dare we shout and think we are so great while hatred spreads
To be or not to be means, choose to be with the enigmatic magic of
the trees.

Don't get ripped to shreds by the news.
You want peace, and peace in the world; be like the trees.
Madness is the absence of the experience of Life itself.
In the news I see only unloving, dangerous dramas out there.
But in the trees interplay and movement I see our uplifting dramas
and operas;
Hidden, unwritten amongst the foliage, waiting for your heart to
bring them to life.

24.9.2017

NATURE AND NEWS
[2ND DRAFT]

Through my window, a fiery, rust red tree dazzles;
Sharing the garden with demure yellow foliage.
Larger trees in multi greens surround under a milk grey sky.
But on my desk, a newspaper filled with the usual madness.
How the hell can sensitive people survive with this ugly 'noise'!
Wake up, I'll have my say; do we here feel the same way?
These gorgeous trees, real and true, for all to enjoy.
While hiding in its leaves, the paper spews lies and ugly dramas.

At the foot of the trees, I see naked babies crawling around a naked mother;
A metaphor for the elemental energy of Life.
The reds and greens are beautiful musical harmonies;
The news doesn't sing; just vomits discordant mania.
How dare we shout and think we're so great while hatred spreads!
To be or not to be prompts that we choose to be with the enigmatic magic of trees!

Don't get ripped to shreds by the news.
You want peace, and peace in the world; be like the trees.
Madness is the absence of the experience of Life itself.
In the news, I see only dangerous dramas out there.
But in the interplay and sway of the trees, I see our dramas and operas,
Hidden, unwritten, among the foliage, waiting for our hearts to bring them to life.

WHERE LEADS FORCE?

Narrator: Topical subject: Not sure what Christmas message is nowadays. Is it: "Peace". Or is it: "Find bargain presents for people who you don't really care about". But, as brainwashed beings, one step up from apes, we can't avoid sheepish, mindless tradition. What about the rest of year? Do we only love our friends and family at Christmas? And did Jesus see into the future, and the huge business to be made by being born on the 25th? Is that why he set up the Retailers Association?

Right. Well first I want to say, that this is only writing.

Which at best, can be enlightening.
And it can be poetic. Though this can get up the nose a bit.
I mean, it won't change the world. I'm just writing about it.
And from a safe desk. Yes, and if pressed, I'd have to say, I'm a coward.
And so most of us are. We all avoid the 'hoo - ha'
As usual, the question brings, what can we do to improve things?

We're up against Greed and Egos. And that's the way it usually goes.
So, sit back, put your feet up, have a cup of tea, or pot of coffee.
Then watch your brain bulge as you indulge in a few choice problems.
Some of folk's quirks which tend to put a spanner in the works!

Today's burnt peel in the pure marmalade of life is this:
Force, in all its forms, including swearing,
Where is it leading us? And before you cuss, "What harm is a curse!",
Take a cursory look at society. All the swearing and violence.
Does it make sense? Violence is non intelligence. Non violence
makes sense. Though I can't see that Ghandi was the man for me.

There are exceptions!! If your perceptions say that things look black,
Like if you're under attack, then let fly, don't die! Hit back!
By the way, this human quirk is part of our writing homework.
And I've been up all night to get it right.
Our teacher's particular, about things extracurricular!

Now for an expert view. Here is the transcript of a TV interview with
David Frost and Sir Reginald Pluss, QC and MT, United Nations
Secretary for Underdevelopment Overseas, which I bought at cost:

Frost: "Sir Pluss.....

Sir P   "Oh, there's no need to be formal. Just call me, Sir
            Reginald Pluss!"

Frost: "Well, Sir, What are today's really pressing problems?"

Sir P   "Well, I've got some ironing to do! Ha, ha. Sorry. Well
            fancy giving the new England manager £6M. a year.
            It won't work. They still haven't learned. You've got to
            teach kids ball skills.

            Ah yes, I see what you mean....well it's the same
            trouble with all these Charities. They throw money at
            Africa and so on, but, damn it.

            They've still got the same old problems. No, you have
            to train people how to farm and how to grow their food".
            Just like kids have to learn their football skills.

Frost: "I hear you criticising others. But what about us? Look at our Army in Iraq and Afghanistan. We are losing whole Battalions to drugs. British soldiers on drugs are being invalided out every year".

Sir P: "Well, that's because they don't like the idea of being killed. They can't face it. And you can't blame them. The time was when, that is what a soldier had to expect. That he might die. But not now. The whole Modern computerised Weapons concept, has reduced the chance of a Soldier dying. So it's harder to accept. I can see the day coming, when the family of a soldier killed in battle, could have their grief filled with pounds and pence. They could sue the Nation. Compensation for negligence!"

Frost: "I agree. Moving from military force, can we go on to violence at home. The growing violence on our streets, among the youth. And the terrible Culture of Bad language across the whole of society. And do have a drink. It's Tesco tea topped with a spoon of third grade Marijuana".

Sir P: "Er, right. Thanks. Ah, bad language. I've always seen swearing as a kind of violence. Swear words are like using your fists or swords. Usually when you are not sure what you are saying. Or when you are angry. Swearing and rage go together".

Frost: "Can it ever be stopped?"

Sir P: "No. You can't stop it! It's inbred. It's what makes this country great. Like Fox Hunting. Or shooting tigers. Anyway, this is all getting a bit bloody serious.

Frost: "So will we ever get back to the old days with less bad language?"

Sir P: "Afraid not. It's in us. Physical violence and vocalising it. Using rude words which you know might upset someone, well, it's dangerous. Exciting. Instead of just being angry and arguing, spicing up your language is fun. And modern life is so stressful. We lead far more complicated lives than ever before. Our brains are overloaded with Junk mail, computer data, advertising, instant news. You know, the Futurist Art Movement tried to print instant News before it had even happened. Now instant, made up News stories are de rigueur.

No wonder people are confused, and there is so much tension and frustration everywhere. I'm getting confused, myself, just talking about all this, Bloody hell, I nearly swore then!

Actually this reminds me of something I did as a boy. You know, boys will be boys. But I was normally extremely well behaved and polite, coming from a Diplomatic family. I was waiting by my father's Mecedes car, in a busy, high road. He was having a meeting with important business friends. And for no good reason, without thinking, I wrote a very rude word in large letters in the dust on the car. I didn't really know what it meant. But I must have spelt it right. My father was furious when he came out, with his VIP friends and they all saw it. He asked me, and I owned up. The rebel in me, was making a stand. Trying to break out and take things in hand. It was a long time ago, and rude words didn't fly around so much. My stab for freedom didn't work. And I have remained in hiding ever since; obedient and polite. The authentic me, of risk, adventure or bust, the fearless me, remains hidden in the dust!

Sir Pluss: [continues]

"By the way, if we are not ourselves, are there two of us. The one we hide, and the one we show? Is it a kind of trick? And does this mean we are all Schizophrenic? Thanks, I will have some tea. Now, I think this is probably all going over the heads of your television audience!"

Narrator: I now want to move on from that TV interview. You got the gist. Let's all go out and get.. .... Wait. Maybe we'd better do the song. Do sing along. But you will need a strong intellect, because it's on the same thing. I don't like Violence. Only Peace. There are exceptions of course. I like to see Millwall and West Han fans making out. And I do like the rivalry between Madonna and Lady Ga Ga groupies. Here's my song: 'Growing Violence Isn't For Shrinking Violets'. I'll sing the English translation from my original English lyrics. And my backing group sing in the Russian. I'm singing it along with my Russian sisters to show that Violence is a worldwide problem. There's a recording with Russian girl singers.

TUNE: *"LAST CHRISTMAS"*
[WHAM / GEORGE MICHAEL] [RUSSIAN GIRL'S RECORDING OR INSTRUMENTAL

VERSES 1 & 2
If you use the sword, you'll die by the sword.
Just being yourself will bring its own reward.
Do the strongest always have a ball?
And do the weak live their lives in free fall?

You just can't afford to hang on to that sword
Just being your quiet self will bring its own reward.
Do what you can and accept what you can't do.
That in itself will help you stay true to you.

CHORUS 2 & 3
We've got to, get rid of violence
But it's everyday that we go on this way.
When will the violence cease?
People need something different.

CHORUS 3
All of you leaders you have consciously lied.
The change has to come from us way down deep inside
That's where the violence just has no place.
That's where peace is gonna shine on your face.

VERSES 3 & 4

If you're stuck in a cage then it don't take a sage
To know your frustration and all of your rage
But all of our great and reliable leaders
Are oblivious, they don't know how to lead us.

We're going to the edge of the cliff like lemmings
As they all sit around like a bunch of lemons.
Their papers, their promises and their fine words
Won't stop violence, their games are just too absurd.

CHORUS 4 & 5
We've got to, get rid of violence.
But it is everyday that we go on this way.
When will the violence end?
People need something different.

All of your plans, won't change anything
All of the efforts of Geldorf and Sting,
All the charities, the U.N. and Bono,
Are just a drop in a polluted ocean, you know

CHORUS LINES:
Stop the violence. Get rid of violence. End violence. Stop violence.
Get rid of violence. End violence. Let's try peace. It's time for tea!
La, la la la

Lyrics sung to Music of : "Zing Went the Strings of My Heart"

When will the violence cease.
When will we have some peace.
We're not Cave Men any more.
Something inside of me,
Feels like it's heavenly.
That's what our inner world's for..

It's like it's fresh as Spring
It's such a precious thing
To feel at peace not at war.
That's how the violence stops
Inside of us it's tops
That's what our inner world's for.

They keep trying force to end it
With punishments, that won't fit.
And keep repeating, endlessly,
"You're a misfit, you're a misfit."

Let this contention cease,
Inside us dwells the peace
Force to stop force is just wrong.
Of course please stop the force.
And go with the resource
I've just described in my song.

One thing will never part.
The love that's in your heart.
Clouds hide the warmth of the sun.
Become a friend of heart.
That's where we all must start.
Then violence changes to fun.
Then peace replaces the gun.

SHORT STORY

GHOSTS ON THE COAST

On a quiet, far flung promontory, along the coast from a Royal Naval port, a young man leans on safety railings, dreaming out to sea. 27, slim, in smart casual, John was lost in uneasy, drifting meditation. A light breeze whipped the choppy waves; a power boat sped past, close to shore, with young passengers in high spirits. On the far, purple grey horizon, a fishing trawler.

Behind him, the sleek, smooth hills, broken up with crops of rocks and bushes, were brushed with sunlight, and ever changing cloud shadows.

Sleek hills of grey blue green under pink cream sky dappled dotted with the checker point pointilist hatchings of bushes grasses and rocks

Over the restless sea, his disturbed thoughts ebbed and flowed; augmented by habitual, painful unease and waves of rage. He looked up at the pale fading turquoise dawn sky, streaked with creamy apricot. If only his bloody inner war would fade as smoothly, he thought. From his chest, his heart, slick slices, of rippling waves of prayer energy swelled up through his stretched throat; a silent begging prayer, and, intense longing; he implored the sun to unfreeze him; to open the doors and defrost his frozen cabinet of fears; and thaw the cruel sore; unlock his paralysis. He wanted the blue of the sky and the warmth of the sun inside him.

Apart from the lack of closeness and the uneasy tension with his father, growing up in the 1930's, in a comfortable home, was sweet and tender. Under peaceful English skies, the in between war years, were full of promise; of friends and fun. For those not caught in the Great Depression, that is.

Just that rippling wave of beseeching had some healing, calming affect on him; like when cream is smeared on a burning sore wound. What he had come to the coast for was already working; the sky, sea air enlarged his inner space, relief from the pain; from the ghosts; however temporary, he was grateful.

It was still early morning, and the light of a hopeful day spread across the coastline. Before dawn, he had fled the city. With a day off, he needed space and sky; to give his ghosts an airing; a break. The train sped to the coast, filled with commuters, students and military personnel; he chatted with those around; there was a university near the seaside town he was going to. He felt the speeding train, a conspirator, on his side, quickening his escape, whipping him to the coast, to kick the ghosts into the sea. In his dis-ease, he hoped the train wouldn't stop, but crash through the station terminus, and dive over the cliffs straight into the sea, drowning his unease once and for all; and exorcize the bad feelings. He felt, all the lost passenger's lives would be as nothing compared to him being free. But the train stopped at the terminus, and jolted him from that imaginary disaster movie. He walked through the town down to the beach and then along to the promontory.

Train; people sailors; life turned around; not free; ants on a project to survive beat off invader; lives altered against will as stream dammed up is forced to change course.

Shrieking gulls swirling in the electric cobalt sky, reawakened his shrill inner noise. The silent prayer was, as he well knew by now, just a temporary lull. Kicking stones in frustration, he turned away, making for the town, needing company. People in Holiday, coastal towns are often more friendly and relaxed than cities.

Maybe being close to the elements, open to sea, sky and wind, helped to open inner doors; be less inhibited, and, less complex.

He walked over to a large coffee bar, busy with students and military people. He got a coffee and sandwich, and went to a table where were two young, pretty girls. "Is this a free seat?", he asked, with 1940 English politeness. "Yes sure", one nodded. They were studying. "Are you cramming for exams?", he asked. "You're dead right", they smiled. "They start in a few weeks", one replied, nodding, with raised eyebrows and a humorous expression of mock disgust, as if taking some foul medicine, but seeing the funny side. "It's that time of year isn't it. I did mine a while back.", John added. She responded, seemingly glad of a break. He was aware that in the city he probably would have got a glare back for being cheeky. But she was warm and friendly. The other girl, got up with her books and papers. "I've got a class. Okay Jenny, see you back at Uni.. Bye".

John and Jenny went on chatting in the cafe, and then walked along the promenade by the sea defences and barbed wire; past military gun batteries, and an old Napoleonic Martello Tower, now a look out post. Suddenly the siren went off. In a few moments, planes were overhead, a air raid attack German bombs falling; the firey flaming Incendiaries nearby. They dropped down and cowered huddling against sand dune banks; he threw a protective arm across her. "They're going for the Naval Port; this is the off target stuff", she shouted above the noise. "The Luftwaffer have upped the raids. It's daily now". A few minutes later the siren wailed all clear.

They walked on. She told him Uni course in English literature and classics studies. But in her spare time she did voluntary Red Cross work.
Helping to pack medical supplies for overseas.
love. He explained that his was a family high on Victorian morals, low on love.
Tendency to seek approval, affection. Hadn't been nourished along with the feeding bottle and milk

Father man of duty, Victorian; John, dreamer, seeing poetry beneath and on the surface. But, conflicts. He still felt like a runner who is impatient to start race, on the line, waiting. Skylark did his own thing; his own matrix nature must too.

His father, a successful bizman and MP used clout and connections to get him into Intelligence Service [Special Ops Section / SOS] And so, he was excused call up to any active fighting service.

At Uni, he had studied Law then switched to music. Wrote songs, lyrics, and short stories. He did some work for West End shows. In intelligence he knew Ian Fleming, who encouraged him.
Had flings at Uni, but insecurities were a wall to getting too close to girls.
Jenny had classes and had to leave. They agreed to stay in touch and meet again.

Taking the time / morning off, he'd got the boost he wanted from the girl, the skylark and fresh air. Now he felt refreshed to go back to city to special ops office. It was off Fleet St. nr. St Pauls. There was a special ops lunchtime meeting to discuss plans tactics for one of the current special cases. He has some paper work. Then a job investigating and tailing a suspect, after lunch.

His team were working on a case, of a suspect double agent. an active field operative in France, who was supplying us with info for use by the French Resistance. Bletchley were involved. Some of it was false info to throw / confuse / waste time of Germans. But too many raids and ambushes by Resistance were being smashed by German army to be just luck. After discussion, the special ops team is a making a move to get proof on their man. Equipment, bugs, cameras, 2 way radio, guns are assembled. His London counterpart also suspected, being investigated; plan to follow him; he is visiting Trent Park, a Bletchley satellite code receiving center, with secret, sensitive docs info. John is selected to shadow. He follows him from his London flat; by tube to Oakwood; long walk, by lake thro forest to the old manor house. set in Nature Reserve, Trent the Royal mansion house was converted and now used by special ops. Popular picnic site; late Spring, daffodils, cows, pine trees, smells. He notices 4 or 5 suspicious men behind trees.

He senses they must be collaborators, double agents, Nazi sympathizers, meeting here, before going into house. The double agents; it double his uneasiness; out here with more than he bargained for. Not just the one spy, several. His fear, anxiety, rising tensions.. Checks on the group of men still talking behind clump of trees. Keeping his distance, he keeps to edge of tree line near mansion, and gets photos of people coming and going from house. He feels the pain and fears of war crystallized inside him, mixed with his own personal war, demons and ghosts. There's an huge explosion near him. A grenade. His rage, frustration shoots up in unison with violent noise. He's been seen. It's the group of men attacking. They toss another grenade. Trees catch fire. His fears and torments are get mixed up together like some painful terrifying threatening cake mixture; just a few local trees catch fire; he is on fire inside; Inadequate, insecure, pangs, shadowy echoes; he knows sharply to get away; but the hot firey forest, is burning inside him too; emotions ablaze, anger at the men; his father, his insecurity;

Fire, shooting, quintessential hot flicking lapping red white flames in forest and inside too; roasting, burnt alive, charred flesh burnt at stake sympathized with Joan of Arc; flames thro trees devastated; how to put out fire, inner and outer? The inner war, battle; needs Water, sea to quench coast, girl, comfort, ease, birds animals shrill cries escape; the explosion, the animals noisy crescendo and inside him too; he runs; being young he is fast; getting away from the agents; getting away from his ghosts, speeding thro the forest / trees; like this morning on the speeding train to the coast. now he is physically actively escaping. He sees now, the agents are not chasing; they go towards the house. He suddenly comes to a clearing, a quiet glade; he is paralysed in shock after all the noise and mayhem in this peaceful, still, idyllic spot; but there is a picnic going on there; a Primeval scene' a mother, and several babies, all naked, climbing around the mother, on a bench. It calmed him down. Fed his elemental side. Or was it a daydream?

Speaks to office in evening on 2 way radio. They instruct that tomorrow John makes his way to the coast, nr Dover. The latest reports say these double agent men are known to be heading any minute to coast there to meet a boat to go to Europe John skirts mansion, hurries past lake, and returns back to HQ. Sleeps there in bunk.

Has a long dream that night. Imagines monster rising out of deep lake attacking him; A three animal headed Chimera type monster, part lion, serpent, goat, breathing blazing fire, the fabled mythological creature, appeared in sky above lake and hovered there, it's body greeny grey flecked with blue and gold. It began convulsions, writhing as if in conflict; from it's body oozed miniature, animated cartoon figures in b/w against blue and apricot sky. some fabled animals, unicorns, snakes, Medusa, Cyclops, angels, winged

Pegasus.....some human, both divided into groups, peaceful and evil; in peaceful group, Jesus, Ghandi Dorothy Oz and Unicorn, Pegasus, angels and there my new student friend, Jenny! In evil group, Ghengis, Bismark, Stalin, snakes, Cyclops....

A lovely tune was playing, "When you wish upon a star", and Dorothy was urging the evil ones to stop their aggressive convulsions. The Chimera monster wrestled and writhed; it got so intense, trying to rid itself of a terrible agony. Dorothy, Jenny, and all the good ones floated off in the sky with that beautiful song. Suddenly, to end it's pain, Chimera swooped up high, then dived down into the forest fire!

Early next morning, John travels to Dover. He makes his way on foot along the coastal road to the spot he was informed. about. A man is standing beside a large rowing boat. John waits and watches, hidden behind a sand dune close to the water. His information told him the escape would be made mid morning. He glances at his watch. It was 10 am. He sees them crunching across the beach to the waiting boat; the 5 men. The same men, double agents, who he had fought with yesterday in the park. He recognized them from their clothes. They greet the man by the boat and wait. John was told, from intercepted signals in code, that the escape vessel would be a motor boat. It arrives and lays up fifty yards offshore. The rowing boat and men start off. John emerges carefully and swims underwater the short distance. He climbs unseen, onto the motor boat, on the far side from the 5 men. Hidden behind a winch, John pulls the pins and lays two handgrenades. He dives overboard. They explode, and soon the boat is ablaze. The crew and 5 agents jump overboard. A fast police launch with Special Ops. agents slows down, and John clambers aboard. And the crew and enemy agents are picked up.

Dry and back in the London office, John phones Jenny. He is given some time off work. The following day he meets Jenny at the same coastal cafe. They walk in the seaside gardens; After the hectic antics, Jenny, like the mother and babies in his dream, calms him down.

TREASURES 5.4.06

Z stood on the landing stage, his bags on the ground around him. A mild Khamsin breeze was blowing. He watched as the Nile ferry pulled away, out to mid stream, and Z waved goodbye to the Egyptian crew. Having finished 2 years in History and Archaeology, he was taking a sabbatical year off university, travelling round Asia, to study, photograph and write a comparative dissertation on great Treasures of the ancient world. Z was a good looking, yet strangely insecure young man. He was at Luxor making for Thebes, to study The Temple of Kings. In particular Nephrates. Partly funding the trip himself, his parents had also chipped in. He had saved up, working in photo modelling and film extra work during free/spare time from his University classes. He used an international visa card which he kept in a flat plastic pouch, on the inside of his trouser leg. He had come to Egypt via Europe, where he had visited a number of places, including Rome and some of Chopin's homes in Paris and Valderama, in Majorca. Z played piano and did some composing. He had arrived in Cairo, taken the Nile river boat and stopped at a few places of interest.

At this time of day, late afternoon, there were only a few people on the jetty. His jet black hair, ruffled by the breeze, was etched against the electric cobalt sky. He shouldered his rucksack onto his wiry, 6ft frame and headed for the youth hostel. There he meets a guy, Q. A fellow Uni student. Next morning, both take bus to Thebes. He sees bright sky, feels light, and inner surges like nature, flood, earthquake. To surrender, get in flow. The scene has a calm mood of history you get in ancient places. Like the Temple Mount and presence of Jesus, a year before. The mood is probably created by our imaginations from what we know about ancient myths and kings, from the past. Suffusing the air with lived in mystery. Clouds begin to spread magically across the dreamy blue. And Z notices / dark figure seems to be watching him behind columns. He tells Q. Q says it's the heat. Q. goes off with a different tour. Z dreams in front of sheer cliff walls, looming up, solid, calm unjudging, just how he wanted to be. lime green with moss and lichen.

As Z waits for his guided tour to start, he sits on a comfortable bench falls asleep and DREAMS: shaking temples fall, dust. Yellow sand, blue sky. Queen Nephititi and her courtiers come out of temple. Festival. Food. Dance with Queen. Folk dance changes to popular. Fred Astaire joins in. Pick self up number. Judy, Gene. Chorus numbers in and around temples. Pyramid slaves. Miss World contest with the Queen Nephititi, Esther, and other imagined ancient beauties

Z comes out of dream. Joins the Guided tour of Pyramids. In underground chamber, he touches a wall, and a connection is made. He taps into ancient primordial life energy. Egyptians knew about electric life current to maintain good health and balance. They held batteries in hands to connect with cosmic energy channelled thro. Sun gods. Into meditation, Z. taps into life energy flow.
Dangerous if knowledge is in wrong hands. Can be used for power/ evil. So simple. Have this energy power. It's what makes us tick. Just remove the barrier, the smoke screen, and we have access, our password to our life energy. Asleep/awake. Power/no power. Active, inactive. Live/no live. What is the barrier that prevents access?

Z feels all this in the chamber. Contact with old tomb where this wisdom is in walls hidden, triggered thro. sensitive Z like electric current. He feels his life. A bright flash of energy, like static electricity / lightning, from Z to down deep in Pyramid; from the tombs and back again. Does it have to be contact only with old things which has this wisdom? Or can we wake up, anywhere. Just ask/want it? As the tour group moves around, Z senses a life energy in human Egyptian form, a being, watching him. Was his earlier dream a herald for future awakening?

Sceptical of that way of living, where people huddle together for friendship, like sheep, not to feel alone, or bored. Blogs, Social Media, forums, profiles, i - pads, photos. People don't really say much @ public events, sports, clubs, etc. People meet for togetherness. But more to life; i.e. Jonathan Livingston Seagull. Can that closeness of friends be like the experience of flying; just for its own sake.

Back to Hostel. Q. is off to India. Next day Z goes back to Cairo. After the Pyramid experience Z has extra awareness. He knows he is followed in the steamy smelly Bazzar. Z over hears U.S. agent, on mobile, pretending to be a tourist. Z chats to the agent; they meet for coffee. Z pretends he doesn't know. The agent F. makes his pitch. "I am recruiting field agents who have a reliable cover. An Archeology student with regular vacations sounds good to me". The pay sounds good to Z. "Okay", he decides. "Er, but only in my Uni holidays, like now" F. agrees. "Of course. Here are your first orders." F. confides to Z; "You fly to Athens in a couple of days. You'll make contact with our Greek agent for further orders. Here is an advance and paperwork.

Meets the greek agent in Athens, who turns out to be a lady, P. Not bad on the eyes! She inducts Z. "I am an English teacher in a local Greek Language school. "That's my cover and I have an assistant, E. who is a holiday rep. The CIA are monitoring the Far East rise in Trade and Armaments. Saboteur tactics are used to damage China and India's trading and Arms sales. P. continues, "The Far East competition is gradually affecting the U.S trading power. Like a python squeezing! We have a large network of sub agents like you, in major countries, who acquire and pass on the information. Projects also include the drugs and ancient treasures trade. That's why we wanted people with your kind of cover." She eyes Z and smiles It's good pay. But be warned. Watch out. There are these gangs of Far East agents out to stop our projects. You're booked into a hotel. Go out and do your archeology studies and in a few days, we'll send for you to begin work.

On the Acropolis Z. sits in the shade of a column, notebook in hand, and day dreams

He dreams of an ancient Greek chorus, musicians, dancers and of a Dark figure in old

Greek form, watching Z, like a spirit of ancient treasures, making sure he does no harm.

Then a group of mysterious Eastern spies attacks the chorus who transform into heroic young men. They fight. They fall off a hill. Z. falls over sideways and wakes up!

FOLLOW ON TALES

A slim girl of 20, Heloise, a gentle soul, in pale lilac grey dress with long gold auburn hair stands overlooking the black Seine on a bridge in Paris; it's a warm summer's evening. Near Calais, the fighting; the French led by Joan of Arc and English. Sweet sounds of running water drown the abysmal menace of the battle. Her concerns; should she marry her love, Abelard, a fine, honest and brave young man, but against their family's wishes? But they knew if they disobeyed and brought shame to their families, the penalty in those days was stoning to death. So they would have to leave the town, far away, to set up together, he a carpenter, she a weaver; a low income, but in love; a simple true love? The river answered her with flashing flecks of reflected golds and browns from the surrounding houses. Yes! No choice. Her spirit flew ahead as she walked to his workshop......

Leonardo walked quickly to his master's workshop. 16 a slim fragile youth, pleasing in appearance; a mane of curly reddish hair, apprentice to Master Piero Della Francesco the famous artist. Through the cobbled windy streets of Florence he ran He was late as usual, busy since early morning anatomical dissections and drawings at the local hospital.
A crisp Autumn day, his mind whirring, full of ideas he was working on. Inventions, research; he took on the Universe; with his genius, the world and all its mysteries was transparent.

Arriving at the studio Leonardo told Piero what he had been working on inventions since dawn. His Master grinned pleased with his pupil's enthusiasm. Leonardo set to work to finish the angel in the beautiful Baptism of Christ painting of his Master. The brush strokes flew, as his spirit flew across the rooftops of his native city........

Up they both flew, across the sky in love, Marc and Bella, in brilliant blues and reds. Above the tragedies of the world; above their own struggles. Their only child, Ida is born in the Spring. He makes money from his art exhibitions. They spend a winter in the country, Marc teaches art to orphans. The cold does not cool their love their passion and interdependence. He becomes embroiled in Revolutionary politics and can't wait to get out of Russia………

J. artist, writer, has to escape the noise, frustrations, the emptiness of his life in the city which is insoluble. He hits on making a visual and audio record, a documentary of some of his favourite architecture, art and celebrities. And a blog on his pocket laptop He makes his way to Rotterdam, in the rain, by train and ferry. He enjoys both the modernity and pre -war style, though not much was left. Rotterdam in the rain! Modern European art fills his senses. And that exultant, exciting feeling he always gets when presented with the new and unknown like in this city now. Leaving London to tour around Europe, was like peeing back the stale uneatable skin of a banana to reveal the luscious fruit within.

Then on to Weimar; the atmosphere so calm, slow; a medieval town where great artists like Goethe lived and worked; J's. creative excitement grew in his chest and belly.
On his European Rail Season Pass he leaves Germany for Odessa. Eisenstein, Eisenstein! The Battleship Potemkin, the steps, gunfire, the pram down the steps; the early proletariat's revolt. J's family escaped from Russia the same year, 1905
In an Odessa nightclub he meets a couple of young girls, K. and S. Drinks, dancing, laughs. J. feels insouciant, carefree, that he hasn't felt for a long time. The threesome sleep at the girl's flat. It's the girl's Easter holidays from University; both studying Literature.
The trio drive in their UZA Patriot down to Baku, Checkov's summer home, now a museum. Spring weather; showers and sunshine. J. impressed and pleased with the girl's literary knowledge. Feels closer to S with her deeper calm and dark good looks.
K more frivolous, light headed, blonde, but still with good common sense.

They drive on from Checkov through Turkey, stopping at several archeological sites, to Istanbul. They explore the city for a couple of days, and spend their last night together. J. unable to commit to either one. The magnetic pull not strong enough for that. The girls drive on back to Odessa and J. takes a train. The claustrophobic

London life was easing, like a thick, noxious smog clearing. Using his on / off season pass, he travels first to Sofiya, taking in the sights. He ignores the night clubs now, needing the freedom of travel. On to Belgrade, to Zagreb [The 007 route] to Ljubljana, then down to Venice where he chances to meet in the bar of his hotel, a widow, V.,glamorous and chic. She is in Venice for a Board meeting of her ex husband's international Beauty care company. They get on, exchange contacts for the future, and J. goes to her room. A sumptuous, erotic end to the day!

J. trains from Venice to Florence; spends several days there. He's especially enchanted with Masaccio Fresco's in the S. Maria del Carmine which he always loved. And the Giotto of St John's Ascension in the Santa Croce. He was surprised at how lively Florence was; the cafes were busy with young students wildly waving their hands, talking about the Italian Elections, Berlusconi, football, their prospects and love lives.
J. fell in love with Ghiberti's fabulous, "Gates of Paradise", Gold and Bronze Reliefs on the Baptistry Doors. The superb carvings wafted relentless magic and charm through his being, his heart. With so many artistic wonders around the planet, old, new, how come such black violent hate is spewed up to make us all sick!
The metallic lustre, the greens and golds of these doors should enter the hearts and minds of men and women and there bring peace. He recorded and filmed the comments of tourists enjoying the spectacle. J's. thoughts electrified his spirits as he stood astonished. And it seemed as if these ancient Renaissance buildings were calling out in gold light across the city, "Fight for delectable Beauty & Love. That's it.

Train to Genova on the Med. Quaint fishing village; now a tourist attraction. On to Monte Carlo. Here not "Beauty" rather, "Millionaires" the watch word; the pervading atmosphere. And here J. is at home with the myriad of famous artists who lived around the Cote d'Azur. Picasso, Chagall, Matisse, Renoir, Bonnard......J. visits the museums of Chagall, Matisse in Nice and Picasso in Antibes. He luxuriates on the beaches which Picasso frequented. Inhaled the magical, otherworldly, fairyland charms of Vence and St Paul de Vence where Chagall lived. Pure Enjoyment.

DICING WITH DANGER

And I Vic, thought I knew everything. Jane stood there against the bar, the pale apricot beach accenting her blue green eyes; but they were filling with moisture. Like a violin, her feelings, like music poured out in liquid passion. She wanted more. Somewhere, her eyes said, is a place right for me. But not this. Even with her friends, with Tom her husband and his hotel business in Cannes, the sun and sand, all that and it was not right for her. The bamboo and raffia screens spilt split shadows across her face. A visual for her split conflicts. She was an adorable creature at the best of times. But now, standing here, vulnerable, frustrated, tearful, it tore at me. I put my arms around her.

They both heard raised voices in the streets behind the beach. It was more rioting. Another fierce demo against the unjust, corrupt government. We heard shots. The police were here again trying to dampen down the mob. Their anger was hot and would not stop. A boy bloody ran down to the water edge to bathe his wounds. Loudspeakers, the police, warning shots. It was so ugly. The pain in Jane's eyes turned to horror. She screamed out, shaking and ran away to the rioting. I chased after. She was running hair wild with the shouting mob, and carried on toward the police wall. Fighter planes screamed overhead. Loudspeaker warnings grew louder, more threatening. I lost sight of her.

I rang Tom at the hotel to warn him that she had gone wild, lost it. Tom got Bill from the bank and they raced to the city centre. They were coming from just north of the riot, nearer to the police wall and might see Jane before me. I rang John in New York and told him what was happening, and added, "They're out of control this time. But it can only end one way and Jane is caught up in it. And she wants to be. She is very upset?"

"Tom and Bill are gonna find her and get her out", Vic told John. "John, it's just a fight against bullies. The government. That's all this is. Always was, John was in his study at New York university between lessons. He had a student with him for a tutorial. Ann, well known to Vic. "John, put her on. Hi Ann. What's the younger generation's take on all this mayhem and rioting," I asked Ann. "You jolly well know what it is", Ann emphasised. "Economic inequality", she went on. "Corruption by those in power at the expense of poor masses. Plus inability to empathise with another's experience. And only think of the self; selfish egos!" "Of course Ann", I agreed. "Yes, abuse of power and all that. They make promises, seduce the masses just to be elected and get hands on the reins."

"And Vic", Ann went on, "Friends and lovers swear to do this, be that, just to get a taste of the honey, and some kind of power. We're all lots of ants chasing around after pots of honey. With socializing it's comfort and satisfaction."
"You're dead right Ann, as usual. Put John back on will you. And keep up the good Sociology work." John, what's it gonna be with Jane?" She's leaking heartache for you still. You know Tom and her are drained out. Your divorce will come through in a week or two. Jane has told you she will come over to New York, because your Uni position is solid. She can find work in the hotel business there. Forget about Ann. She's too young and you know it's unethical. A student. You know deep down you still love Jane."

"Yes you're right Vic", John knew. He had to take the plunge. Jane's craziness in Cannes sent the message. Hammered it home. "Vic, get a message to Jane somehow. I know, I know you're right. I've been too mixed up. Vic, Vic, I love her!" Vic said, "I'll send Tom a text. He won't hear me over the rioting. He'll tell Jane when they get her out of there.

FAMILY RESEARCH

Andy was reminded of a rare history book belonging to a family in Russia. It fetched thousands at auction. He remembered the cover was embossed in dark olive green with ancient Celtic symbols. In Russia for example, one hears in book circles and in social media searches of many such finds. And so in all countries with long histories and rich culture. Except in America.

40 year old Andy, a documentary filmmaker was embarking on a venture covering European cultures. A comparison and analysis of selected artistic and political projects. This was his cover. And he speaks fluent German. His family from Hamburg area. As an agent working for M I 5 Andy and several other European secret agents were still tracking any ex - Nazi members alive, in conjunction with the Weizenthal office, in Vienna. But they were also commisioned to keep a check on the activities of extreme Right Wing, Nazi party sympathisers.

Sees details in paper of old German family photo album up for sale in Christie's Berlin Auction House. Interest aroused. He wanted more details about his grandparents and their part in the war. When younger he had tried to track down his German family survivors. With only mild success. A few aunts and uncles and so on. Some of his family, he knew, died in Russian labour camps. He goes to the sale room on the day for further information and to check out the photo album. He sees it is a mix of high ranking military and private German families. Is shown proof of provenance. He wants to find photos and text of some of his family in the war. He recognises two names in the album and some resemblance to his father's family.

The bidding is too high for him, but he finds out who bought it and arranges to meet In their hotel. A tall, smooth cultured man and his wife. He was also researching his families.

Andy showed him the two photos and asked if he knew anything. He didn't, but suggested he contacted Archives at the Museum Deutchland Historich in Weimar.
He makes an appointment. The following week, his first free time, he Trains to Weimar. It's a light showery the next day when he leaves the hotel. He senses the culture in the city of Goethe, and feels secure. He also suspects he's being followed or watched. As the guidelines dictate, being one of the regular hazards of his profession, he pretends to look in a corner shop window. It happens to be an art gallery showing Chagall prints. He checks and sees a suspicious man in raincoat who also stops to look in a shop. Andy goes to a cafe to reconnoitre and watch. The raincoat enters and sits on far side with newspaper. Andy waits, then gets up to go to the bathroom. He checks coast is clear then slips out the back door. Down a garbage strewn alley and makes his way to the Museum.

His appointment is with a pretty young German lady in Archives, Marie. "You're interested in tracing some relatives, right? As you can imagine we have a huge database, mostly on microfilm and computer files. I'll need a family name to start." The search began. The upshot was a few photos of family members and names. Easier than he thought.
And being a state funded museum, no charge, just a suggested donation. And a bonus. Andy and the young lady museum assistant had got along so well, she agreed to meet him on her next free day

The rain had stopped. But the raincoat man was still there. Andy turned and walked toward the man to confront him. The man ran off. Andy decided not to chase him. In this business, agents were two a penny. And he was a bit tired from concentrating on files and microfilm.

Andy trained back to Berlin that evening. Aware of possible tapped phone lines, he sent a coded message to H.Q. They replied to Andy, to all local agents that Nazi cells were active and also on the defence. And the raincoat man was probably just one of them.

Andy followed up on the family photos and names, but got nowhere.

Andy also had a Berlin contact for messages. Joseph ran a rare, antique bookstore.

Andy was filming near the shop and went there. Messages were conveyed inside books.

Joseph knew Andy was researching his family and showed him the history book with the Olive green cover and Celtic designs. It was modern German history with photos.

As Andy thumbed through he recognised some faces in group photos of Nazi Party members. And some faces actually matched the photos he got from the museum. He showed them to Joseph. "It was going to be more than likely", Joseph remarked. "Now I've given myself extra work digging these people up," Andy moaned. "Haven't we got enough chasing ex Nazis!" "Only got yourself to blame", Joseph laughed understandingly. "You'll want it. That's 50 Deutschmarks reduced from 175. They exchanged some messages and Andy went his way.

He met Marie the museum assistant a few days later. Early morning they drove to one of his relatives whose photos and address had been found. Not there presumed dead. No forwarding address. He tried another address, also near Berlin. The same. Not living there. Presumed dead. Over a late lunch in an open air cafe by a lake, Andy tells Marie about his passion for European Arts and his documentary. She is fascinated.

Marie knows one of auctioneers well Karl, at Christies and arranges to meet for dinner later that day. Karl has his 35 year old daughter with him. Refined, cultured. Recently separated. Marie slightly put out by this unexpected appearance. Andy shows Karl the family photos in the book. Karl agrees to help out if he can, but won't get involved directly himself. Christies must be seen to remain impartial. After dinner, Marie and Andy wind up back at his hotel.

"CHARACTER: This guy had everything. Spread sunshine and laughter, life and soul of party.... but, a beautiful bird in a gilded cage. Because, he had an Achilles' heel; a sensitive, painful glow, glimmering inside him, would become a raging fire, when he had any aggro or upset with people. The smoke and flames changed his sunshine to black pain. Would sharing love dowse the fire...? LOCATION: In a forest, with tall, slender trees, he wandered, to heal his pain. OBJECT: To heal wounds and become whole again. THEME: He walked in the forest, outside the city, wanting to be healed, and have his inner fires put out. He had walked in many forests, many times, for same purpose. This time, as he walked, the tall trees slowly bent down around him, caressing and hugging him. He wasn't scared. He wanted it. He felt the healing. Then he walked on, and there, by a lake, a lovely girl, having a picnic with friends, invited him over. They chatted, and he felt his fire growing less intense. She had a lot of common sense and humanity. Then laughing, she pushed him in the lake. He noticed his fire was almost gone. "Of course, we always need some glimmer of fire", she said, as he came out the water, "it must never go out completely. Just so it's under control and not painful"

"CHARACTER: "Isosceles, the no good, two faced Triangle, was a new break away, Slob Unitarian, who had few morals, and broke most of the Ten Commandments, including some, even Moses didn't know about! A six foot, 20 year old country lad, he was the weed gardener at the main Middlesex Uni campus. Despite being a bit of a screwball, he was friendly with some of the staff and students there; often chatting to one professor, a square, conservative egg head, who was an Ovoid shape. Isosceles played bass in a retro rock and roll band at weekends, in local pubs. He was trying to make out with Betsy Catsy Love, another Triangle; she was a Performance student; but it was a Menage a Trois, as Sid, a five foot Pyramid, was after Betsy too. LOCATION: Sid and Betsy on the way to a party in car. OBJECT: How best to resolve a love triangle. THEME: Betsy, the triangle wore a red dress, Sid the Pyramid read the Sat Nav, and Isosceles saw red. So he fired round mortar shells at their oblong car, speeding down road. He missed on purpose, just expressing his jealousy. At the party, Isosceles tried too hard with Betsy, went off at a tangent, and so lost her. If you're only two faced, and got an insecure hypotenuse, the girl will go for the solid, three dimensional guy instead.

CHARACTER: Big Issue' street seller, a squatter with mates, but still retains passion to do more than work and share in his community. Creative skills; songs with lyrics, poetry, short stories, etc; a lyrical soul. But also has desire to help improve the current social status quo. Member of his local squatters working committee; Regular posts on local borough Forum. A Michelangelo imprisoned slave, struggling to escape from out the marble stone. Several close mates; one girl shares his dual dreams of creative work and practical changes. They go to have meeting with Housing Dept, taking with a petition to have legal property possession, plus samples of their songs, and writings, to prove they are not just drop outs.

CHARACTER: Warm, friendly guy, 30's, wide circle of varied friends, a fighter, with emotional scars, which he has risen above; inner city social worker, so, he has good empathy for his client's struggles; frustrated with red tape; and also a frustrated creative artist, who knows the word 'create' lies buried and stifled in the word, 'bureaucratic', but hasn't yet found a way, financially, to change his life style.

"LOCATION: 1950's / 60's Retro cafe; juke box, guitars on wall; burgers; photos of Elvis and others. In a trendy, tourist coastal town; present day. Popular with the young and old. Many elderly enjoy memories. Occasional Live retro bands; some clients dance; jive and twist.

"LOCATION: Lively market'; trendy shops and stalls, by a canal; a tourist spot; fishing, buskers, barges, a soap box spot for political speakers. A film is being made there. Noise, crowds, smells from the cafes and food stalls.

"LOCATION: Pub; live bands, and audience spots for poetry, song and comedy. Up market, not working class; crowd includes students & ex university, some published, some on the circuit, some professionals, mixed with those struggling lower down ladder.

OBJECTS: I hope this is what you mean by 'OBJECTS'. Here's a list: Time Machine; Trendy Yacht; Flash sports car; Box magic tricks; real live Robot; High speed train; Bottle shampoo; fags; bottle coke; vacuum cleaner that talks; bicycle that can go through any object; lawn mower; a Genie; a type of Pandora's Box.

THEMES:

[1] Each person in story is either male or female Dictator or a Saint.
[2] positive reactions to everything;
[3] negative reactions;
[4] Each person, or some, are made of a material / element, i.e. wood, metal, water, air, fire, gold, etc., and talk according to what made of; water talks in flowing style, wood, metal in hard, brief way, fire in angry, passionate style, etc.
[5] Some people have conscience that talks to them.
[6] Trying to reform, be good from a bad past, or bad past life.

STORY idea: Rhythm of contrasts

There's too much somethings in the world now. Noise, thoughts. Nice to occasionally, have nothing to fall back on. To relax. To just be, and feel the wind and rain, the smells The air. And even in something, there can be nothing, to enjoy. Like in the eye of a storm. And if you don't try hard to get something from nothing, then you will enjoy the 48 % of nothing, which is itself, everything. A greater pleasure than sipping a Pina Colada on a tropical beach. Too much something, like over thinking creates noise inside. There is enough noise on the outside. Over thinking is a kind of pollution, waste matter, and is non productive.

2018 SHORT STORY 'BLENDING'

Watching Judy Garland and Robert Walker again in 'The Clock', I am still blown away by this beautiful portrayal of love blossoming over one weekend, and the risks of such an accidental coming together. It depicts that long forgotten romantic, sincere true love so keenly expressed in the romantic popular songs of the day, Compare that with the dying love of today as exemplified by the divorce rate. What percentage of the world's population experience this true lasting love?

In The Clock, a World War 2 film, she's a secretary and he a soldier, on leave in New York; their burgeoning love to become a life long and sacred plant. I soak up their friendship vicariously as if strained through a muslin.

But this was 1944, when love was more often genuine and lasting; at least until 1945. Today, closeness is a mishmash a hodgepodge of contradictory motivations; an exotic fruitcake that becomes stale and boring. And how much is the real article; how much lust; how much companionship; and how much is a divorce nowadays!

Anyway, they are both from the countryside; both naive and simple hearted, so they don't have that intellectual constipation, or gift of the gab in disagreements which so often eats into innocent love like acid dripped over an apple crumble.

With false and true love in mind, I give an example of an affair of a case history from the files of The New York Marriage Bureau:

Two students, a boy, B. a biology student and a girl, F. [F. for short] meet at a university dance in the Jitterbug competition. which they won. Part of the prize was to dance up on the high stage. They were doing good with multi double somersaults, through the leg slides, and over the back spins series, which could have put an Olympic Gymnast out of work

He was showing off with a particularly complex bit of foot work, when his legs got mixed up at speed as he threw her through a series of across the back spins, and they both fell heavily from the stage to the dance floor. There was a loud crash and shouts. But both his legs were broken in several places. He writhed and screamed on the floor. His partner F was lucky, as she fell on him and escaped with a only a number of broken vertebra, shortening her by several inches; meaning she could only kiss the average guy by standing on a step ladder.

In hospital for a long stay of treatment he was tormented with pain from his mangled legs but also tormented by the brunette nurse [K] on his ward. Heartache is not a symptom which medical science has come to grips with. The most common prescription remedy found to work is a bottle of malt whisky followed by 2 fried eggs

Needless to say, his double pain, legs and heart brought them closer together.

That and a passionate love of Jazz [1931 - 1932; pre Django, post Miles. Suffice to say their romance grew, though hospital romancing is taboo. They determined that theirs would succeed even if K had to leave nursing So it was after months that B, the boy, was discharged from hospital to Convalescent home where K got a job The unspoken bond between them grew stronger, deeper. At one point they pooled their collection of jazz vinyls and their passion melted the plastic, creating one very large LP. Love was fusing them together at much the same speed..

Eventually he got his discharge. At the same time K left too, and they set up together. She enrolled in medicine: after care. They agreed their love was meant to be. That everything that happened in their lives was to bring them together. So okay pretty average love story so far!

One evening they were both luxuriating and relaxing in a restaurant when an admirer sent over a bottle of wine. They chatted about can such a good thing last. But then they had a short spat over nothing. She was going to leave in a huff when she saw his sleeve had a ketchup stain and cleaned it while he gazed at her and said to her, "You've got brown eyes!"

But for the Ketchup the tale would have ended here. It was after midnight when they left. No buses. They hailed what they thought was a taxi It turned out to be a mail van. The friendly driver J gave them a lift and took the couple home to meet his wife G. They ate talked and laughed When marriage came up the young couple said, the war made it difficult; not knowing how the fellow would come back, and if at all. But the elderly couple, the driver and wife said that if people thought of all the things that could go wrong they would never do anything and if both were in love, they shouldn't wait.

The couple left, mulling it over. By now, in 24 hours, they were really digging each other. K had to go to her medical college to explain she had to spend the day with a soldier on his last day of leave. But they got separated on the subway and didn't know how to meet up again. K went over to the Armed Services Missing Persons but didn't know B's last name. They were both absolutely frantic and heart broken.

But some policemen suggested B to go to where they first met, the rail station. And K was there! They hugged and kissed on the escalators and ran off to the city marriage bureau. After enormous effort, having to get blood tests and be back in time, they were wed. They are seen next having a meal in a diner. K begins to cry about the wedding ceremony...."It was so, so...ugly!" The scene in their hotel room next morning is superb! They share unspoken looks of close understanding as she pours his coffee.

He is going back to army camp and probably to war to fight. And he asks her not to worry or think too much. And she replies, "You're coming back. And you know how I know. Two days ago we didn't know each other. It's all meant to be. They kiss tenderly.

He goes off; and she walks out slowly through the station

Lightning Source UK Ltd.
Milton Keynes UK
UKHW010829280220
359503UK00001B/34